XIII
BLOODY ROSES

XIII
BLOODY ROSES

Commissioned by BUYA PUBLISHING INC.
and
Written by **TYLER HAUTH**
Illustrated by Various Artists

*"We want you to visit our State of Excitement often. Come again
and again. But for heaven's sake
Don't move here to live..."*

-Tom McCall

Tales

Written by Tyler Hauth

A Note on the Art

The illustrations depicted throughout this book including the cover art, are all images commissioned by BUYA PUBLISHING INC and created by various artists from around the world. Each artists unique contribution to this book provides context to accompany the images within your own mind.

Together, XIII Bloody Roses has been brought to you as a beautifully illustrated anthology, we hope will occupy your bookshelves for years to come.

Illustrations & Artists

Cover
Art by Ross Malet

Portland Underground
Nazi Cop
Suicide Bridge
Art by Roval Tarroza

Kids Kill
Art by Constantine Hlyvlias

No Breath
Art by Arika Chamberlain

Asylum Avenue
Forest Park
Black Water Blues
Seven Against the World
Otherworldly
Art by Igor Beltrame

Threader
Art by Sergey Shirobokov

Lone Fir
A Portland Nightmare
Art by Anna Vaks

Shanghaied *by Roval Tarroza*

Portland Underground

Portland, Oregon (1884)

Eliza peers into the dark and suppresses the wave of shivers that normally follows. At half past noon, the sun is the worlds brightest lantern and only the Shanghai Tunnels are evil enough to keep it at bay. The damp smell of the river lifts up from the soggy passageways. The harder she looks, the more it appears like the black is alive and moving. Is something down there?

A squeal of wind (she hopes it's wind) breaks the last of her courage and Eliza leaps to her feet, scrambling away from the hole gaping in the alleyway. She runs back to the mouth of the lane, comforted by the sound of the bustling street behind her.

Is it true what Mary and Nancy say? The twins like to tell stories, but they're not the only ones Eliza's heard talking about the Portland Underground. She's overheard sailors warning one another not to get too close to the tunnels. And people do disappear. William's father went drinking one night last Fall and never came home. They whispered for weeks that he hadn't fallen in a ditch or run off. This whispered that he'd been taken.

There are people down there in the tunnels. She knows that for sure, because her father is one of them—and although he says it's boring and not worth talking about, he also warns her to stay away from them. Because he's lying about the first part. It's not boring down there. It's dangerous and scary.

It's not just her father that uses the tunnels. Bad men use them, too.

Foreign sailors that don't have teeth and will hit you just for looking at them. Strange men who don't speak English and come from distant places Eliza's only read about in books, where tigers and lions are as common as cats and dogs. They leer at you if they catch you staring. If you're not careful, they'll crack you over the skull with a mallet or pick you up, screaming, and carry you off to their curious ships and that'll be the last any American ever sees of you.

And if you're a strong man capable of being sold into slavery? Then they'll capture you and lock you up in the tunnels until a slave ship comes. What will you do when you wake up with no land in sight and the waves shifting under your feet, but work for fear of being thrown overboard if you refuse?

When her father goes into the underground, she never sleeps until he comes home, even though he insists he'll be fine. What if he has too much to drink before he goes? What if someone hits *him* over the head? At twelve, she's a proper lady now and wants to behave and be good. But there's something about the tunnels she just can't shake. How deep do they go? How many are there? Which bars and shops are connected to the system, and how many exits are there?

Could you get lost down there? Could someone shove you in a cell meant for barrels of wine and forget you were there?

Are there skeletons?

Opium dens? Like Mother says?

Worse things—things she's not supposed to think about until she's married?

She turns back onto the street and starts for home. Father's meant to leave for England tomorrow. That means he'll be in the tunnels tonight. Walking alongside the strange men that come from places she can't pronounce, who sail into port in the morning and are gone by afternoon. Men who don't even know or care about laws. Men who steal things (*people*) and never get caught?

Father's always shifty when she asks what he does down there. Even Mother can't get anything out of him. She's heard them through the floor at night, arguing about it. Father always answers the accusations the same way. *This is what I do for my family. What else can I do? Captain Riggs isn't a man you say no to!* If pressed too much, he claims to be packing the boat. But don't they load ships up with supplies on the docks?

Still, people have been going missing more often lately. It's not just William's father that hasn't come home. Charles didn't know his father was missing for months, because he thought he'd sailed for a distant port and only known something was amiss when he didn't come home. The crew said Charles Sr. was never on board. The same thing happened to Alice, just about, only her father was just sailing down the coast and so they knew he was missing without so much time passing.

She looks both ways before darting across the cobbled road, leaping over a puddle of muck and landing lithely on the far sidewalk. Her shoes are white and she has to keep them clean. A pair of draft horses pulling a cart laden with great crates stuffed with cotton and tobacco catches her attention. She pauses, watching the lumbering beasts pull all that weight and smiling at the coachman. He nods at her absently, watching the busy road.

At home, Eliza talks with Mother and makes a show of writing in her diary at the table. Then, when Mother gets busy with laundry, she flits upstairs quiet as an owl and pulls her pack out from under the bed. She checks her window for the fourth time since she woke up this morning, fiddling the latch *just so.* She pushes it open, listening carefully, still suspicious it might squeak. But it doesn't. It's quiet as can be.

She reaches into the bag, careful to listen for her mother's footsteps on the creaky stairs. A pair of pants she borrowed from James a few weeks ago, and a shirt that George gave her in exchange for a pair of her panties (she never asked what he wanted to do with them, and more importantly, he didn't ask what she wanted to do with his shirt, either). A hat to hide her blonde hair will finish the illusion that she's counting on creating—that she's not a young woman but a boy. There's some grease on the axle of Nancy and Mary's carriage that she thinks will help conceal her pale face and make it look like she has a mustache, or a bit of facial hair.

The most important thing she has is a four inch letter opener that's sharp enough at the end to prick blood from your finger. She doesn't want to use it, but it seems foolish to wander into a place like the Shanghai Tunnels and not have something for an emergency. If someone tries to steal her, they'll have another thing coming.

She shoves the pack back under her bed and tidies up her room. Father normally spends the day before he goes at the bar. She looks out the window, wondering if she might catch him coming back, but she just sees a pair of old men with rakes on their shoulders hobbling down the lane.

The stairs creak and she turns from the window, clasping her hands neatly in front of her and trying to look anywhere but under the bed.

Her mother comes blinking around the corner. Her hair is tied up with a piece of string and her face has a smudge of dirt on it. "Eliza, where've you been today? Mary and Nancy came looking for you earlier and I worried."

"I was looking at the horses on Main Street."

Mother smiles gently. "Are you worried about your father, again?"

She pretends to hear something interesting outside and turns. It's easier to lie when you aren't looking at Mother's honest face. "No. Will he come home from drinking soon?"

"I told him to be home for an early dinner." Eliza hears her crossing the room. Mother's hands fall on her shoulders and she lets herself get pulled back into a hug.

She turns in her mother's arms and returns the hug. It feels good to be wrapped up in a safe place with the weight of what she's going to do tonight pressing down on her.

Mother grabs her chin and pulls her face up suddenly. "Are you all right, dear?"

Eliza tries to break the grip of her strong fingers but only succeeds in hurting her jaw. "Ouch!"

"Well I didn't ask you to twist your head like that," she says snootily. "What's wrong, Liz?"

Eliza steels her expression and glares. "Well you've just about twisted my head off my shoulders!"

Mother balks. "Watch your tone, missy. Do you want to ruin your father's last day on shore? I don't want to have to tell him that you've lost your manners."

The threat is enough to silence her. She doesn't need to get in trouble. This argument is the opposite of what she wanted. "Fine." Her temper is still too hot for her not to add, "no reason to accost me in my own room."

Mother puts her hands on her hips. "You just be glad I'm feeling gracious. I don't want your father to have to worry about you being out of line while he's gone."

Eliza watches her go, still fuming. What'd she have to go and start a fight for? No reason she should have grabbed her like that. It's not respectful. That's not ladylike. For someone always preaching that you need to act like a lady, Mother often does things that are far from reasonable.

Of course, following your father into the seedy Portland Underground isn't exactly respectful or ladylike, either. Neither is sneaking out of your room after sundown. But she's about to do both of those things.

But she thinks, perhaps, now isn't the time to throw stones.

A few hours later, she hears Father coming in the front door and skips down the stairs to greet him. Her dress flies around her and she fancies she looks a bit like a fairy. The mirror set against the far wall across the stairs proves that to be partially true. She smiles at herself before she bounces onto the landing.

"You're chipper," he notices, red faced from walking and drinking. The more Father drinks, the redder his face gets, until, eventually, he looks a bit like a ripe tomato.

"It's your last day on shore." She pouts, just the right amount, and crosses her arms. "You've been gone all day."

"They don't have bars on the boat."

"They don't have *me* on the boat, or Mother."

He frowns, looking like he hasn't considered that before. "Well I'm here now, aren't I?"

She follows him into the kitchen, where Mother is banging around pots and the smell of fresh yeast rolls is heavy in the air. "Will you be here for dinner?"

He checks his pocket watch, squinting for a long time, like he can't quite make sense of it. "It's nearly four."

"Dinner is at *six*." She knew to expect this. But she has to confirm he's—

"I've got to load the ship. It'll take most of the night, darling." He puts his hand on Mother's shoulder. She turns, tugging on his tight ponytail and rubbing her hand through his scruffy beard.

Eliza sticks out her tongue when they turn to her.

"Don't you want to see your parents in love?" Mother asks.

"I don't want to *see*."

Father laughs heartily and grabs for her. She could get away, but she lets him win and joins the hug. The timing bell rings after just a few seconds, and for a moment, Eliza hates it more than anything in the world. If the timing bell hadn't rang, they would have kept hugging, and maybe...

But no. That's a stupid, childish thing to think.

She's not a child anymore.

Mother jumps and extricates herself from the familial embrace. "I always miss you."

Eliza turns away from his smiling face. If he always misses them, why doesn't he spend more time at home? "You're going into the tunnels again tonight."

Mother tenses, but Father looks like he was expecting this. He nods gravely. "It's my job. We have to load up the ship. We're taking—"

"I don't care what you're taking!" Eliza snaps. She starts to say more and stops, realizing from his pursed lips and narrow eyes that she's upset him. She gives him her best glare instead.

Mother turns from the oven. "She's been haughty today."

"I'm not haughty. I'm a lady."

Father smiles. "Girls are supposed to be haughty, especially when they're your age."

"But I'm not *haughty*." She suppresses the urge to kick him in the shin. Perhaps that'd be a haughty thing to do.

"You're definitely something." He's still smiling, and so she knows he isn't mad anymore.

"I don't want you to go into the tunnels. They're frightening. People get stolen in them."

Mother claps her white, dusty flour hands to her forehead and Father sighs gently.

"I mean it. Don't you know about William's—"

Now he actually is mad. He snaps and points his fingers at her like a revolver. "That'll be enough. I know all about William's father."

She holds her ground defiantly. "And how about Alice?"

He turns his back and leans on the counter. "I know about him as well. These silly stories don't have anything to do with the Shanghai Tunnels, Liz. The only people down there are sailors. Men just like me who just want to get the job done and set sail."

But she knows when Father turns his back that he's not telling the truth. She can tell in the way he puts his shoulders. He doesn't like to look at her when he lies. If he doesn't want to tell her the truth, *fine.* He may as well force her to follow him down there.

She knows to trust her gut. And her gut tells her that something funny is happening in the Portland Underground. Her gut tells her that the stench of rotten river coming up from those black tunnels isn't natural. Her gut tells her that the shifting shadows hold some kind of malice in them.

There's something wrong in Portland. Tonight, she plans to discover for sure what it is.

She walks to the sweet shop with Mary and Nancy after dinner, only half listening to their gossip. There's half an hour before dusk, and that means there's time to kill before Father leaves. One of the best things about being friends with the twins is that you very rarely have to actually chime into the conversation. They talk ceaselessly, all day long. Sometimes it's enough to drive you mad.

Right now she enjoys their voices undulating between the creaking carts and clopping hooves that float from the thoroughfare. A pair of men in fancy suits pass by on the opposite street, and Eliza notices one of them pointing toward an iron grate that can be lifted to access the tunnels.

"Let's cross the street," she says, interrupting Mary in mid-sentence. Without waiting to see the twins faces, she darts across, weaving through the light traffic without stopping.

They come puffing after her, feet clattering like a shower of stones tossed from a rooftop.

"Eliza!"

"You'll lose us and get left alone!"

She waves their pale faces framed by bobbing brown curls away and points. "Let's listen to those men."

One of their favorite activities is eavesdropping on strangers. They perk up at the suggestion.

"All right." Mary picks up the pace. The men slowed a little at the sight of the grate, but they're still moving. Mary waves her hand impatiently, and Eliza darts after her, pulling Nancy along by the hand.

"They're looking into the tunnels," Nancy gasps. "Father said—"

"Don't be such a baby," Mary gasps. "Listen."

The taller of the two men is talking rapidly and loudly. His voice carries easily in spite of the street noise.

"You'll find the worst kind of depravity down there. Half of em' want to be taken, I think."

The shorter, fatter man stumbles on a broken bit of sidewalk and curses. "City is falling apart. I swear—"

"Thing is, there's plenty of ways to get in and out." The tall man talks over him, not even looking to see if he's fallen. "Even if they blocked up some of the tunnels. We've got the ships waiting. What's to stop us from unloading tonight?"

The fat man runs to catch up, scuffing his polished black shoe and nearly tripping again. "The crew is set to leave in the morning? Loyal men?"

"The man I've got in mind has done it a dozen times or more. Good man. Ruthless."

"We'll have a dinghy at the shore. How many will he bring?"

He shrugs, as if the question doesn't matter. "Sometimes more than others. Never know until he shows up. Most he ever got was 9, I think."

Mary looks over her shoulder at Nancy and Eliza with shocked blue eyes.

Eliza holds up her finger. "Shh."

"Mostly strong men?"

"Normally a smorgasbord. Some of em' are barely fit for more than fun."

The fat man grunts. "What the hell is a smorgasbord?"

His friend sighs. "Just have the dinghy ready. The rest of the crew knows when to board. Slaving free men in the America's is risky."

Eliza, sensing the danger, grabs the back of Mary's arm and plants her feet on the sidewalk a moment before the portly criminal turns to check the vicinity. His eyes scan over the trio of girls as if they're sidewalk chalk—looking for police, or at least adults—never suspecting that they'd have the gall to listen to a strangers conversation.

He turns again, and his reply is lost in the clatter of a mules tapping gait. Eliza's left with a shocked and shaken pair of twins that can barely understand what they've just heard.

"Isn't *your* father sailing for England tomorrow, Liza?"

Her ears are still ringing from what they've heard, and Nancy has to ask the question twice more to snap her out of the daze.

"What's that, Nan?"

"She said, *isn't your father sailing for England tomorrow?*"

"Oh. Yes." She points across the road, at the shifting sign that reads: SWEENEYES SWEET SHOP. "What do you think he'll give us for three pennies? That's all Mother gave me."

"We each have a nickel," Mary says proudly, reaching into her pocket to retrieve the shiny silver coin. "That means thirteen cents altogether."

Nancy isn't so easily distracted. "Eliza! Did you hear what those two gentlemen were saying?"

She starts across the street, nodding, still fuzzy headed. "I don't think they were gentlemen."

"They were talking about the tunnels!" Mary recalls snappily. "And stealing—"

Nancy hits her hand quickly, "*shhh!*"

She lowers her voice. "They were talking about slavery! Stealing people and stuffing them in the tunnels and picking them up in boats."

Eliza feels Nancy grabbing at the back of her dress and turns before it rips. "What?"

They're standing just outside Sweeneyes Sweet Shop, now, and Eliza wants more than anything to get her hands on a good piece of licorice or maybe even a chocolate bar. But Mary and Nancy are staring expectantly.

"I don't think the ship he's on does things like that. He's going to *England*, you know?" Who is she trying to convince? The twins, or herself?

"Well how many ships are leaving port tomorrow?" Mary wonders.

"I bet not many," Nancy says unhelpfully. "They could be talking about your father's ship, Liz! Do you think your father would be on a *slaving ship*? A ship that steals—"

"They aren't!" Her eyes get watery even though she isn't sad. She crosses her arms and spins, deciding on the spot to leave the twins where they are and walk home alone. If they're going to suggest something like that about her own father, then she doesn't want to be friends with them.

Nancy and Mary cry out together, running after her. "Wait, Eliza! Wait!"

She tries to twist out of their grasps, but the two of them overpower her. "We're sorry."

"Yeah," Mary nods. "Real sorry. We didn't mean it."

Eliza glowers at them. The sweet shop seems less important now than it did a few moments ago. Now all she wants to do is go home.

"We just thought it was funny," Nancy whispers. "Your father is a sailor and he's leaving tomorrow and those gentlemen—"

"They're not gentlemen," Eliza growls.

"Those men," Nancy continues, "were saying that a sailor was going to steal people and put them on a boat leaving port tomorrow. Isn't that funny, Liz? Isn't it weird?"

Eliza sighs. It is weird. And she's felt that something was wrong for weeks. She's sensed it longer than that, maybe. Because the one thing she hasn't said to anyone, not even to Mother, is that Alice's and Charles's and William's fathers all went missing on nights that her father was down in the tunnels.

They all went missing on nights Father was meant to sail for England. On nights he was loading up the ship for Captain Riggs.

"I guess so." She bites her tongue. Can she trust them? "But I have a plan. I know it's not my father. I know it's someone else. And now I know I'm right to be worried, because there *are* bad people down in the tunnels."

"Does *he* go down in the tunnels?" Mary asks breathlessly.

Eliza nods, not trusting her voice.

"Gosh." The twins look at one another, wide eyed.

Nancy asks, "What are you going to do?"

Eliza decides there's no point in lying to them, too. "I'm going to follow him down there tonight and make sure no one hurts him."

For a moment, neither of them speak. They stare, slack jawed, as if they haven't heard her right.

Mary breaks the silence. "You'll get dirty."

Nancy nods at her white shoes. "You'll ruin them, your mother will be cross!"

"Your dress will never come clean." Mary sniffs. "It's not ladylike to go into the tunnels. It's dangerous. Didn't you hear those gentlemen —"

"They're not gentlemen!" Eliza barks, loud enough to turn the head of a pair of ladies walking on the other end of the street.

Mary raises her eyebrows. "Fine. But you heard them, didn't you?"

"They could try to hurt my father. What would you do?"

They shrug. "We could tell the police."

Eliza suppresses the urge to roll her eyes because she knows it's not nice. "That's not going to work. And anyway, I'm not asking for your help. I'm just telling you because you seem to think he has something to do with it! But he doesn't. I know he doesn't. And I'm going to see what he does tonight and then I'll know for sure and mother and I can be happy and know that he isn't a bad man, he's a *good* man."

The twins look at one another conspiratorially. "It's called circumstantial evidence, Liz. Haven't you read the paper before? It's what the court uses to determine if someone is *guilty* or *innocent*."

Now Eliza does roll her eyes. She can't stop it. "I'm going to go home. You're not being nice."

This time, the twins only look on worriedly as she walks away.

Father leaves at dark. She hangs on him at the door, realizing it's a baby thing to do and not caring in the way that you sometimes realizes you're being rude or mean but can't keep yourself from acting that way. Sometimes, Eliza thinks she's not much different than a cat that slinks in an alley and hisses at a dog, no matter how friendly or calm the dog seems. Sometimes she just has to hiss and there's nothing she can do to help it.

That's what it feels like right now while she hangs on Father's arm and whines that she doesn't want him to go.

"Can't someone else load the ship?"

He shakes his head gravely. He's dressed nice, in a new pair of boots and clean pair of britches and a nice white shirt that will be stained and sorry by the time he gets back from England in a couple months.

"You'll get awful dirty down there," she says, thinking of the twins and hating herself for sounding like them. "Look at your nice shoes, Father. You'll get them all ruined in those stinky tunnels. Can't you let someone else do it, please?"

He looks at Mother for help, and Eliza feels her cool hands press around her shoulders and groans. "Fine! I'll let you go, and I hope no one clonks you over the head with a mallet and tries to steal you away. That's what could happen down in the tunnels."

He shakes his head, smiling gently. "You're the sweetest thing."

She scowls, not feeling sweet at all. "If that's how you want to act. I hope they don't steal you away, Father, we won't even know where to look to find you and Mother will have to marry the milk man and then he'll be my Father and everything will be ruined!"

She flies upstairs at full speed when they start chuckling, only looking back to send her evilest and most angry scowl flying like an arrow. By the time she reaches the landing and starts down the hall to her room, they're hugging and Father is hefting his bag and opening the door.

It's dark out; when he steps out of the dimly lit candlelight and into the night, he seems to disappear from view entirely. Eliza pauses at the top of the stairs, wanting to try one more time to convince him to stay, but she knows it's futile. He never listens to her. He thinks she's just a little girl who doesn't know anything.

Now that the idea is in her head, she can't get it out. What if Father is responsible for stealing people? What if he sails on a slaving ship full of stolen men and women? What if *he* hits people over the head with hammers? What if he ply's alcohol on tired workers and then drags them into cages? Eliza thinks if she went into the tunnels and saw her father pulling a drunk man out of a cage and kidnapping him, she'd go so crazy they'd never be able to get an explanation from her jabbering mouth.

Mother steps out onto the porch to see him off, and that's when she breaks for her room. There's only a few minutes now. She rips her dress off, kicks her shoes clear into the far corner, and throws the borrowed pants and shirt on, feeling like a boy and kind of liking the idea that she might be able to run around in the road and skip straight through a puddle rather than around it and not get scowled at by a busy body from Mother's needle club.

Last, she bundles up her hair, ties it with a piece of old string, and jams the cap onto her head. This is the important part. If her hair falls out of the hat, anyone with a brain would know she's a girl and not a boy. She doesn't know if it's illegal for boys to have hair as long as hers —her father has long hair, after all—but it seems to only be allowed if you're a sailor. And little boys can't be sailors.

Eliza pulls her window open and leans out of the frame, letting her feet pop up off the floor so she can look further. Mother's just seen Father off. She watches his shape walk into the street and listens for the click of the door being closed.

Mother always gives her a while to sit by herself after she gets mad. By the time she knocks on her door to talk, she'll be halfway across the city. At least that's what she hopes.

She turns in the windowsill, pivoting so she's looking inside rather than out, and pushes away. She shoves her feet into the trellis, destroying the vines and ivy but not really caring. She hangs all the way down before letting the window go, trusting the old lattice to keep her safe.

It does. She scales it quickly, jumping when she's a few feet from the ground. Then she scans the street. Father's made it further than she thought he would. He's already nearly to the end.

She runs after him, desperate to keep him in sight. If he gets away, she'll never be able to find him again and then it'll be months of worrying and wondering if he's a bad man that steals her friend's parents or if he was taken by a bad man or if… or if…

She swallows dryly and checks over her shoulder as she closes in on him. Could there be something worse in the Shanghai Tunnels? Something that feeds on the dark and drinks in the shadows and smells like the old, rotten, stale water? Maybe it chews on man bones and cleans its teeth with the fingernails of the hands it rips off for sport; Maybe…

She slows when the tall shape takes a left at the end of the street. This way leads further from the city center. She's never gone far in this direction. It's a bad way, a way Mary and Nancy would shout at her for going. But surely it's safe to go for now. Safe because she's with Father. Even if he doesn't know it.

The letter opener feels heavy in her pocket. She grips the handle, as if for strength, praying again that she doesn't need it. The hat feels awkward on her head with all her hair bundled up beneath it. The brim comes up a little and she yanks it back down, checking worriedly over her shoulder again. What if Mother came running down the street, screaming her name? Father would hear and then she'd be caught. It'd be a disaster.

But Mother doesn't come down the street. No one yells for her to come back home. Father continues walking further from the city center, toward the wharf, and the further they go the more uncomfortable Eliza begins to feel.

A bar with a large, open window seems to draw Father's attention.

He pauses, twenty or thirty paces in front of her, and she matches his change of pace by pretending to study her shoelaces. She looks up while she's kneeling, watching him carefully.

His eyes are fixed not on the bar, she realizes, but on the space between the bar and the building beside it. It's too slim an area to be called an alleyway, but that's the only thing she can think to call it. She figures there's probably nothing there, nothing besides an old stray tomcat, probably, or some rats.

Still, he starts toward it, not even bothering to look as he crosses the road. Eliza looks for him, but that proves to be unnecessary. The only thing of note on this street is coming from the bar, and her father seems to have no interest in joining the revelry.

He pauses in the slim alley, looking over his back once, as if only by habit. His eyes pass over her and she feels her whole chest seize. There's not even enough time to worry. He looks back, progressing further into the side street, pausing halfway into the dark hall.

He bends, lifting something on the ground, and seems to step into the earth itself. Eliza watches him go, holding her breath, and the moment his head dips below the street and he enters the underworld, she charges across the road to join him. She knows better to believe he's disappearing, like some kind of cheap, curious magician. No. He's stepped into a hatch that leads to the underground. He's entered the Shanghai Tunnels.

A dim light flares from the open portal, seeming to come from nowhere. She makes the front of the alley and glances into the bar through the open window. Smoke and lamplight spill out, revealing a disheveled but crowded room, full of cursing, mumbling and shouting.

A pair of men just in view of the window sit with their heads together at the bar. Each have a mug in their hand, and they're passing a small vial of clear liquid as she watches. The bar is loud enough to conceal the sound of her hurried rush, and so she doesn't try to keep quiet.

There's not enough time to keep watch. Out of the corner of her eye, halfway down the alley, the light shining from the hole is fading. Father's climbed down the ladder. If she follows too quick, he'll hear her. If she waits too long, she'll lose him in the sprawling maze that stretches like the roots of a thousand year old oak under the city of Portland.

She looks into the hole, scrunching her nose as the smell of the underground assaults her. The light flees like a thief and she takes the plunge without considering how scary it is to lift herself over the open grate and step down into the dark. She can't afford to be scared, or slow. She's not a frightened girl anymore. She's not in a dress. She's in britches and a shirt. That means she can be brave.

Her hands land on the cool, slick iron of a simple ladder and she scurries down into the dark.

She breathes through her mouth, deciding the sound of her puffing through the dark is quieter than the inevitable noise of retching that would result from smelling the world she's descended into.

While the street is paved, the underground is wet and muddy. Pools of tepid water make it impossible to be quiet. Fortunately, the tunnels are full of curious echoes and it's hard to tell where any one noise is coming from. The dripping of water from overhead morphs with the skitter of little creatures and the stumbling and rolling of carts overhead and it makes a kind of dull noise that makes listening almost impossible.

She navigates by following her eyes. The tunnel they've dropped down into is mostly straight, and every fifty paces or so, there's another grate looming from another street or corner of the city and it lets in a wash of moon and streetlight. That, coupled with the lurching shadow and flickering light that marks Father himself, is enough to keep her from being plunged into the complete black.

A muffled conversation makes her heart seize up inside her. She passes a pair of rooms, one after another, and glances inside of them fleetingly, straining her ears to try and listen over all the noise. It's too dark to see into the rooms, and the carefully constructed gap between them is suddenly growing wider.

She skips forward, heart beating hard enough that she can hear her pulse beating in her ears. The conversation booms and peaks—she realizes it's coming from a room just ahead and stumbles, almost freezing, but Father's moving quicker now and the light is fading. She can't stop. She can't avoid it.

She plows forward, cringing away from the side of the wall that opens to the room with men in it, hugging the dirty, wet wall along the left side of the tunnel. She can't help but look into the dank hole; if not for the voices floating out of it, low and grumbly, she'd never know there were people inside it.

"—why would I pay, I'll take what I want and she can't stop me."

She catches a glimpse of the reply and shivers at the sound of the cruel, cold voice: "Could right kill her and no one would catch us, lucky we brought her down—"

She loses the conversation, and suddenly, loses the light at the end of the tunnel, too.

One moment, Father's shifting form is bobbing along in lantern light. The next, just as she's straining to hear the bodiless men discussing stealing from this unnamed woman, he's gone.

She nearly calls out. Terror washes over her in a sweet, cold sheet and her legs turn to jelly. Without the light, it's impossible to tell how long the tunnel goes on for. A hundred feet? A thousand? A mile? She tries to remember how far she's come and draws a blank. Has it been five minutes, or thirty?

She starts to run and forgets to breathe in through her mouth. She inhales deeply and gags on the rancid, reeking air that fills the underbelly of Portland. She lands in a freezing, cool pool of old water (she hopes it's water) and soaks her britches almost entirely. The floor almost goes out beneath her—she falls into the wet, unyielding wall face first and gasps painfully.

But she keeps running. The light didn't fade or wane—it disappeared entirely. Did someone hit him over the head? Did something grab him? Was there a dark room along the tunnel with a quiet man inside? Was this faceless, nameless, perhaps fleshless, and legless, and armless man lurking there for hours before someone finally came to be taken?

The thought of it almost cripples her. She starts to slow so she can reach into her pocket and take out her letter opener, and slips on a patch of mud. She flings out her hands to try and balance and a shape appears in the near complete darkness as if from nothing. It materializes like a fog, first just a flash, then a whole silhouette that takes the shape of a tall, threatening man.

The man-shape lunges and she has time to take a stinking, rotting breath of air and scream before a great hand claps over her mouth and another wrestles her into position so that an arm can be wrapped around her throat.

The figure picks her up easily, lifting her off the ground like she's nothing more than a crate to be carried to a ship. Like she's nothing more than…

The arm tightens around her, she kicks, tries to punch, scratches at her waist to try and reach for the letter opener, but her pockets are somehow too low, lower than they should be. She remembers, faintly, that she isn't wearing a dress. She's wearing pants. Pants that belong to a boy.

Why is she wearing pants that belong to a boy?

When Eliza wakes up, she thinks she's still in the Portland Underground for a long, frightening moment. And then she feels the world shifting and sloshing under her, and she sees the beaming sun coming through slats in the floor above her and hears the crashing waves and smells an open, sea smell air that's nothing at all like the awful stench in the Shanghai Tunnels.

Something tells her all at once where she is, and the realization locks her whole body solid. The dread from before, running through the dark tunnel after Father, comes roiling back in like a great cart laden with a hundred casks of wine. She feels the hot, choking fear and starts to stand, starts to run even though it's dark beneath the ships deck and she hasn't yet made out the room around her.

She brings her hand up to claw at her throat, imagining that strong arm locking around her windpipe, remembering that big hand clapped over her mouth. Her hands fly and her fingers stretch and a hard, cold chain yanks them back into place. The cruel metal cuts into her wrists and she cries aloud, screaming.

A voice, low and close, draws her panicked eyes and she thinks if she could die from fright, she would.

"You don't want to scream, girl. That'll bring them into the hold. We don't want them in the hold."

Eliza jumps and squints, trying to make out the accent, trying to see the woman that's lurking in the dark beside her.

"Hello?"

Chains jingle and a shaking hand takes shape as the world rocks and her eyes adjust to the dim light around her. Eliza grabs for it, blinking confusedly. A black hand. How can it be a black hand?

"Slavery is illegal," she mumbles as the hand takes hers and squeezes. The Civil War ended decades ago. She's learned all about it, memorized all the important events. They fought to end slavery. Mother said they were free now, that they weren't slaves anymore, that...

"Oh honey," the woman says sadly, "nothing is illegal in the Shanghai Tunnels."

Padded Walls *by Constantine Hlyvlias*

Kids Kill

"I reckon some families are just cursed," Arnold says feebly. The detectives eyes shift thoughtfully above his handlebar mustache. "Cursed?"

"Seems like there's something black with that family, that's all I'm saying."

He blinks. "That family?"

Arnold sighs. A slip of the tongue, brought about by his internal desire to be anything *but* a member of the Yates clan. "My family, then. All right? That what you want? Want me to admit they're my blood? Well don't I know it. But I've never even kicked a dog, let alone drowned a pair of toddlers or shot a woman in the face, or tortured…" he stops himself before he says too much.

Barnie grabs for his pen and scribbles something on his stained notebook. "Let's start with the toddlers, then. Rachel was just a girl when that happened, am I right?"

He groans. These detectives are all the same. They think they get it. But they don't. They want to start with the crimes. But you've gotta start a long time before that if you really want to understand what went wrong. Someone doesn't just wake up and do murder. It's a thing that takes a long time to build up.

And Portland might just be the perfect place for that kind of insanity to fester and breed. In fact, Arnold has often thought that Portland is the only place in the world that this could have taken place.

Where this could still be taking place.

"What's the matter?" Barnie presses.

Arnold gestures weakly. "That's not where I'd start if I wanted to understand what happened here."

Barnie eyes him sourly. "Didn't realize you was an investigator."

"I'm not." Arnold smiles. "But I know a lot about my family. More than you'd believe. And I know they've got some sickness deep in their mind, and I know something else about them, too. Something you won't believe. Something that's true about even me."

He raises a disheveled, overgrown brow. "Something I won't believe? Why's that?"

"Cause it's crazy as a rat with rabies," Arnold says flatly. "Because it's so damned insane you'll probably write down on that paper that I'm an unreliable witness and that someone ought to be investigating *me*. But it's true. Every word of what I've got to say is true. Even if it is impossible."

Barnie leans back in his chair and taps his pen on his notebook methodically. A square, white clock ticks behind him, nearly in tune with the tapping of his pen. The metal, rusty table between them shakes a little as he tilts forward, dropping all four chair legs safely on the ground again, and puts his meaty elbows down.

"Let's just see about that. Anyone who reads these case files—" he thumbs at a pair of boxes stuffed with police records that date back well before 1978 when Rachel, Arnold's 11-year-old cousin, pushed his sister Natalie into a duck pond at Laurelhurst Park and watched her drown to death "—would be able to tell there's something wrong with them."

"There is," Arnold says, trying to keep himself from hoping that Detective Barnie might be different than any of the rest that he's tried to tell his story to over the years. Because hoping only makes it hurt worse when they stand up, looking at him with that half concerned, half fearful expression people get when you do or say something that makes them think you're insane, and make a quick excuse to exit the room.

"Well go on," Barnie says, looking behind him at the clock. "Spin your tale, young man."

At 54, with a receding red hairline and glasses the size of coke bottles, Arnold hasn't been called young for a long time. But he takes the comment in stride and starts at the beginning. The real beginning— not 1978, when Natalie was murdered, or two years later in 1980, when Rachel drowned the neighbors little girl in less than a foot of tepid water in the backyard swimming pool, not even over a decade later, in 1992, when Rachel hired someone to murder a girl she was jealous of.

"I guess it really started in the mid-century. Back then, Portland was still trying to figure out what it wanted to be. Could be a dirty place, at times. Not like now. Didn't have a mask on yet, you see." Arnold nods to himself, liking the way that sounds. He'd phrased it differently in the past, before finally landing on that metaphor. Because Portland wasn't just city, not like New York or Boston or Las Vegas.

Portland was a live thing that breathed and had a heartbeat, and if you nicked it in the wrong place, a gush of gore would spew out of its belly and you'd find yourself wishing you were anywhere else on the planet. Bad things had happened here, more bad things than just about anywhere else. There was a reason for that. Although not many people would ever believe it.

"When you say mid-century—"

"I don't mean the 21st or the 20th," Arnold explains, and Barnie scribbles furiously as he confirms the date. "We're talking 1860s. Before Ford has its assembly lines and before Ronald McDonald owned the world. Damn, to have been alive back then. Imagine being able to take a deep, happy breath without choking on that damn smog that just about hazes the whole city over."

Barnie nods impatiently.

Arnold scowls at him. "Anyway. To try and point the finger at Rachel just wouldn't be fair. The Yates have been bad since before I can track us. No one talks about it, but just a while before she pushed my sister into that duck pond, her momma got shot in the face with a shotgun."

Barnie jolts. "What's this, now?"

He shakes his head sadly. He's got no expectation for these policemen to be anything other than foolish and useless, and somehow, he's still disappointed at just how uncertain they are about his family's history. You'd think an investigator would, you know, *investigate*. But that never seems to be true.

"You heard me. Don't nobody ever want to talk about Grandma Daphne and Grandpa Noland. Nope. It's like you can just sweep that whole affair under the rug and just say, *well golly gee, I don't know why Rachel turned out so rotten*. She was raised by rotten stock! That's why. We all were."

Barnie looks up at the camera that's jutting out of the far corner of the room like an unwelcome erection and gives it the bird. Whoever's monitoring the video probably doesn't appreciate that. But if he doesn't blame them, he'd have to blame himself, and that wouldn't be too fun.

"You're not the only department that don't know any of this shit," Arnold says, almost forgivingly. "Half the folks I talk to are ignorant."

He scowls at being called ignorant. "You know we'll be fact checking all this, right?"

Arnold laughs gaily. "Course. And you'll find it easy to confirm most of it."

"Most?"

"No man alive can confirm the worst of it," he says darkly. "You'd have to run tests. And no one is going to strap me down to a table and poke me and prod me and take my blood, you can be sure of that. Short of that, maybe even God himself can't confirm it. Some things, even he can't see. Least that's what it seems like."

Barnie fixes him with what he probably believes to be a hard stare, but what Arnold thinks is a cheap second rate attempt at a steel expression. He'd tell him as much if he were pressed, but figures it's best to keep quiet about that observation for now.

"Anyway. That was Rachel's Grandma and Grandpa. Mine too, just on the other side. I didn't see them as much as she did, you know. They raised her up like their own. On account of Rachel's momma, Delilah, kind of being a floozy."

"She was a prostitute?"

Arnold shrugs noncommittally. Who knows what she was, other than her? "Guess so. That's what started up that mess, I guess. At least on the surface."

"But what do your Grandma and Grandpa have to do with Rachel's momma getting shot in the face?"

"Well Grandpa Noland is the one pulled the trigger," Arnold says plainly, like it's obvious. To him, it is obvious. Who else would have shot her, if not Noland?

Barnie leans in his chair, balancing it on the back legs again, and whistles sharply. "Boy howdy."

"Caught her in the act in their own home with a strange man," Arnold recalls. "Least that's what he said."

"You're telling me this happened before 1978? And that Rachel was present?"

"That's right. I imagine it was late in the year of 1977. She lived with Noland and Daphne full time, of course. I remember Noland saying something or another such that her momma being a prostitute, she'd be better off dead."

"But I thought—"

"Right," Arnold interrupts. "Whoever heard of someone getting blown in the face with a shotgun and not dying? Darnedest thing, and maybe not even for the best, her surviving it. Life was hard for them all after that."

"Noland went to prison?"

Arnold runs a hand through his thin hair, nodding. "Died a ways back. Long time ago, I guess, some people would say. Doesn't feel like much more than yesteryear to me, though."

"And Rachel stayed with Daphne and her momma after Noland went to prison?"

"Yep." Arnold pops his lips on the *p*. "Changes the way you think about things, at least a little, huh?"

Barnie doesn't answer, but the look on his face tells Arnold that it does. To a lot of them, Rachel was a monster that had no motive or reason for being bad. When they learn more about her upbringing, they soften toward her a bit. But when they learn the truth—the real reason she's rotten—why they're all rotten—they can't face it.

When you think of little Rachel and all the evil things she did—

hell, killing his own damn sister, and what else would make a man hate someone more than that? —the word evil comes to mind. But she was only the spawn of evil, and what she had in her was a shadow of what she came from. And most importantly, it wasn't her fault.

"But 1977's a long time after the mid-19th century," Barnie observes, somehow leading him on.

He holds back a sarcastic round of applause. "That's right."

"So what's this got to do with—"

"I'm getting there." He roots around in his pocket and pulls out a pack of cigarettes. Puts one of them in his mouth, without checking Barnie's expression to see if it's all right, and lights it up. He inhales heavily and then breathes out a big cloud of smoke.

Barnie tugs on his mustache and looks at him distastefully. "I quit smoking three years ago."

He offers the pack of smokes and grins. "Want one?"

The portly detective breathes heavily through his nose and grumbles dispassionately. "Not supposed to smoke in the station."

Arnold sucks in another deep breath, holds it for a moment, and exhales loudly. He doesn't put out the cigarette. "Where was I?"

"The mid 1800s."

"Right." He takes another drag. "Ever heard of the Hawthorne Insane Asylum?"

Barnie stares uncomprehendingly.

"Opened in the early 1860s," Arnold explicates, recognizing the look of abject confusion because he's seen it a hundred times before. Cops don't seem to know shit about anything other than handcuffs and handguns these days. Even detectives. "Guess it was the first in Oregon. Didn't have state hospitals back in those days, of course. It was a private practice. Just about the only place to put lunatics if you didn't want to just let them run amok and do crazy shit."

He scribbles frantically for a while, and Arnold waits until he looks up expectantly to continue.

"Our forefather Henry Yates got himself a job at the asylum within a couple months of it being opened. Called himself an orderly but I reckon that was just a polite way to say he was a nurse without making him feel embarrassed. Nursing back then was a menial job, you gotta understand. Nothing like today. No schooling to speak of. Guess he probably was just about like a janitor, really, if you really wanted to get nitty gritty with it."

Barnie motions at him with the pen. "And you can substantiate all this? You've got records of some kind?"

"Ayuh," Arnold says agreeably. He's got lots of records. More than old Barnie would ever want to see, probably. Took him the better part of a decade to grab this cat by the tail. By the time he finished, he found himself wishing he'd never begun. But this kind of horror has a way of pulling at you and forcing you to keep walking the dog. Not like watching a train crash, but like walking along a train track and realizing if you get off, you might just go insane or die.

"Lots of vulnerable people in an insane asylum," he observes eventually.

Arnold feels his expression go dark. "That was the idea. Henry was, uh, how should I put it..." he actually falters, not remembering his normal phrase and not wanting to make up a new one. The story's been worked over in his mind enough, now, that he doesn't want to mess it up.

"A fucked up individual?" Barnie tries, seeming to sense exactly where the history is going.

"That'd be a fair assessment. But he was only a pawn in that game of chess."

"Someone else was up to no good?"

Arnold ignores him and points at the camera. "They've got my bag. Wouldn't let me bring it inside."

"No personal affects while you're being interviewed." He sits up straighter and his considerable belly pushes against the table. "Don't dodge the question. What'd he do?"

He wags his cigarette playfully. "I already got this. Want to give me the bag, too, so I can read something for you?"

A look crosses the big man's face that tells Arnold if they were someplace private, where he could get away with it, he'd probably *batter the witness*. Instead, he looks dryly into the corner and shrugs.

"Go ahead and bring in the bag, Martha."

He smokes while they wait. Barnie studies his notes. After a minute, a thin, severe looking woman with short hair brings in his bag and looks at the detective for direction.

"Well go ahead and give it to him," he barks.

She does. Arnold thanks her and takes it. He fishes for the diary, an old, tattered thing with a lock on the leather bound cover that someone broke a long time before he found it in the attic of the Yates ancestral home in North Portland. It has a way of sinking to the bottom of his bag, as if it wants to hide.

Finally, he finds it.

"Jesus, that thing's old."

"About 150 years, near as I can tell."

Barnie gapes at him. "You mean—"

"Want me to read it? Maybe it's best from the man himself. Henry wasn't so smart, but he could write decent."

Barnie licks his lips nervously. "Would we be able to get a copy of that?"

Arnold laughs. Others have asked, and he's told them all the same thing. "Go to Hell. You want me to read it, or not? You're not going to believe it, anyway."

He scowls and makes the *go on* motion at him.

He reads straight from the book, skipping a few of the early entries on account of them not being as interesting:

November 3, 1863: All this hard work coming to fruition makes me feel that I'm not wasting my life after all. Dr. Hawthorne told me it couldn't be done without my help. Imagine that, Dr. Hawthorne himself casting praise and recognition upon me. It's good business, that's what Pop would say. If he could see me now. But perhaps it's best he can't. I believe there's something worthwhile to pursue at the end of all this, even if lines must be crossed to achieve it. It's how I've always felt. Dr. Hawthorne is a genius. What we've done here... when the world can see it...

The asylum has more than enough patients to see this through, and the State wants almost nothing to do with these cast-offs. Gibbering and jabbering lunatics, most of them. They scream, but I am not convinced they can feel real pain. Most of our subjects are severely stupid to the point of being incapable of speech. If only they could understand! Then, I think, they would not scream from fear and pain but from excitement and hope! What we could do for them! What we might do for them all!

There's progress being made. Dr. Hawthorne believes we're closer than ever to creating a serum. We will change the world. If these poor, insensible souls could only have use and provide pleasure or perform work. If only they had a mind at least as intelligent as a good fox hound.

November 8, 1863: It's been a relentless week. Dr. Hawthorne upped the dosage, my memory fails when I try to recollect exactly when—three, or perhaps four, days ago—and the results were catastrophic. Their violence was incapable of being controlled. They destroyed themselves. I've buried them each in unmarked graves. That corner of Lone Fir might be full before we're done. But we will persevere. Dr. Hawthorne is a great man. He refuses to give up.

November 12, 1863: Alas! A lunatic has begun to understand commands. Senseless and speechless before, but now capable of listening and understanding. It has worked! A breakthrough. After such a dark week, I feared we were losing faith. So many failures, so many mistakes. This is science. This is medicine!

She will listen to anything we order. Anything at all. Dr. Hawthorne let me have my time with her, and having such a willing lunatic at my command was better than any amount of money. I think I will ask him to let me keep her, if she survives the coming weeks. I deserve a pet for my sacrifice, for my work. She has been here for a number of years, mute and unvisited. It seems her family has abandoned her. Just as well! Now she is ours, and useful again. Perhaps Lincoln will end the slavery of intelligent and speaking men. Perhaps this awful Civil War will be for nothing. If Dr. Hawthorne is allowed to continue—and it seems that no one can stop him, not if I am around to defend his honor and intelligence—perhaps there will be no need at all for it.

November 21, 1863: She has died. But there is more to come. Our serum works better than before. Our dosage is no longer guesswork. Many senseless idiots have begun to understand words and follow commands. The state of their bodies after repeated doses is no matter. There are so many of them, so many subjects, that Dr. Hawthorne is not so concerned about the lesions. The muscles remain intact as long as the eyes. Our longest, a young man barely of age to drink, has been awake and alert for nearly a week! Dr. Hawthorne believes the possibilities are endless. I am apt to agree with him, great man that he is. If only the world could know what he is doing. If only they could see his brilliance.

Arnold licks his fingers to turn the page. He glances up at Detective Barnie, knowing what he's going to see. His eyes are wide and bloodshot. His mouth is slightly open. His pen is forgotten beside him.

"I warned you."

He snaps his jaws closed and swallows. His throat lunges awkwardly. "Of course. Is there more?"

He nods grimly. "Probably a hundred entries, but I only need to read you a few more. Do you want to stop? Perhaps I can explain the rest without—"

"No." His eyes clear a little, and he nods, as if to puff himself up. "I've heard worse than this. Go ahead."

"Next date is December 2nd," Arnold says. "Not much different happened in the time between. Same shit, different words."

Barnie cringes. "It went on for that long? Is this some kind of prank?"

"No." He rubs his finger down the old page, stained yellow with age. He feels the weight of the book carefully. "No. This isn't a prank. It's true. It's true in the sense that there's a record of Henry Yates working in the Hawthorne Insane Asylum during these years. And there's proof of those victims being buried in Lone Fir Cemetery. Someone dug one of them up, once. There's... there's a lot of other things that don't add up here, Detective. A lot of weird things going on in Portland. And..."

Barnie leans forward. His belly strains against his button down, threatening to bust a thread. "And?"

"And I think it all began here," he says weakly. "Or there, I mean. In the asylum. With these damned... experiments. Tortures. Whatever you want to call them. I think it poisoned this whole city to its core. I think…" he stops, not wanting to say the last part. Because the last part is where he always loses them.

Barnie wipes a bit of sweat from his brow with the back of his meaty arm. He looks up into the camera, almost to check that it's still there. Suddenly, he remembers his pen and grabs it in surprise. He starts to scribble in his notebook.

"Go ahead," he says brusquely, a policeman and a detective again. "Read the rest of your book."

He does.

December 2, 1863: The violent idiots are the most interesting, for not all of them are so insane that they cannot talk or be reasoned with, even before the serum. One such man of considerable temper, who walked into a pub and killed a dozen boys with a hatchet before he was taken down with a revolver, has become a most interesting subject.

The altered serum Dr. Hawthorne is testing on him has proved promising. He's developed no lesions, and remained intelligent enough to carry on a conversation even directly after an injection. I believe this is the breakthrough we've been waiting for. It seems, perhaps, that the initial intelligence of a subject can affect how capable they remain after they've received a treatment. I wonder if Dr. Hawthorne realizes the implications, as I do. He is a great man. A genius. A visionary. But perhaps he does not see what could be done with someone truly intelligent.

Why does it have to be lunatics and idiots that we test on? Why can it not—but no, perhaps I will not even write that here, in my deepest confession. Dr. Hawthorne would not like that. It would threaten him. It is not wise to threaten a smart man. Not unless he is defenseless.

Arnold pauses again, wetting his lips. "It goes on for years."

Barnie tries to talk three times. Each time, he chokes up before he can get it out.

Arnold waits a minute, and then adds, "Couple years after this, a visiting physician's report stated most of the patients at Hawthorne's Asylum were abusing themselves. Imagine that. Seeing abuse and figuring, oh, these crazy folk must be doing it to themselves. You can check that one out, Detective. Look it up. Report is in the public record."

He holds up a hand, like hearing it hurts. "I will." His eyes narrow and he hardens himself. "When did it end?"

He offers the diary to him, something he's never done before and perhaps will never do again. "Take a look."

Barnie glances at it distastefully, like touching it might make him dirty.

When he doesn't immediately reach for it, Arnold throws caution to the wind. "Want to know something awful?"

He stares. "I already do."

"Something more?"

He shakes his head. "No. But go ahead."

"1862, records show Hawthorne married. Woman named Ella Murray."

"So?"

"Only lived a few weeks into the marriage. You can look it up. Died under strange circumstances. Never had a proper funeral. Was buried quick. Like they didn't want anyone to see her."

His face turns green and he looks away. "I can't read it. I don't want to touch it. Tell me where it ends, Mr. Yates. Tell me where it ends and we'll fact check this... this tale. And if you're lying to us, I'll arrest you. Misleading an investigation, falsifying records. There's something I can get you with."

He's heard the threats before. They never come through with them, because once they start to check, they realize every bit of what he's said is true. At least the parts that can be confirmed. And because once they make enough noise and really try to figure out what's going on, about half the time, they end up disappearing.

"I'm not lying."

"Good." He nods to himself. "Good. Now what happened to Hawthorne?"

"He died in 1881, I guess. But not before, according to Henry Yates's diary here, they perfected their serum."

He writes something, and then looks up curiously. "But what's it got to do with Rachel, and all this mess we're trying to put to bed today?"

Arnold laughs. "I'll have to read one more passage if you want to know that."

Barnie considers. For a moment, Arnold thinks he's going to let fear rule him. He thinks he's going to shake his head, *no*, and thank him for his time. That's happened before. Sometimes, the threat of awful knowledge can make a man so scared that he'll purposefully avoid knowing it, even if he has a fair chance. It happened during the holocaust. German and Polish villages not 10 miles away from concentration camps pretended like they didn't exist. Like they didn't see the smoke tracks or hear the wails, or smell...

But the fat detective holds out. He nods curtly, and says, "all right. Go on."

He shows the huge stack of pages that span between the last entry he read aloud and the one he's going to, now. "Nearly a decade passed between the last entry and this one. But you'll get the gist of it."

August 3, 1873: Today, I am a new man. To know we've been at this research for so long, to know all that Dr. Hawthorne has lost, and all our tribulations have been for this—makes my heart warm. There can be no great forward movement without sacrifice and hard work. That's Dr. Hawthorne's words, not mine. There were times, I would not admit to this aloud, but here, perhaps it is safe—there were times when I thought, maybe, we would not succeed. That dark year of 1868 was almost the end of us both.

I have received my first dose of the serum. My head hurts, but my body has never been stronger. I've been awake for four days; the desire to sleep is nonexistent, as is the desire to eat. My mind is sharp. My heart pumps slow, even if I run fast. It is time, soon, to expand the subjects. I am that first step. A volunteer. It has won me a great deal of respect from Dr. Hawthorne.

I will bring the kids to the hospital, soon, and we'll administer their first doses. To have the world's greatest children! The Yates name will live forever. Dr. Hawthorne, perhaps, has a lasting legacy. And soon, so will we. As the benefactors of a new age of medicine, where sickness, disease, and disuse are a thing of the past. It will be my name that is written alongside his in the history books.

Perhaps. If things go well. It will be my name alone.

It ends there. Arnold looks up to show that he's done. There's more to the diary, dense bits of information that read harder and tell less. But that bit—that bit there—is the key to it all, he thinks.

Because he remembers getting the shots when he was younger. He remembers the old chest that the vials came out of. The syringe, glistening wetly with a drop of yellow liquid. He remembers the way it burned when Grandma Daphne shot it into his veins, and how awful he felt afterward. Sick and dizzied, confused for weeks. Finally, coming out of the haze and knowing that he was different. No longer human.

The same formula that Henry Yates took? It seems unlikely.

But similar? Undoubtedly.

He's never had the fits of rage of violence that the diary details. So someone—someone in his own family, perhaps—worked on the formula after Henry Yates and Dr. Hawthorne died. To what end? It was never mass produced, of course. No papers were ever written. There's never been an article describing the experiments that took place at Hawthorne's Asylum. Probably because Hawthorne knew they'd be jailed for it. And that his legacy would be ruined.

And yet...

Someone is still working at it.

Are there other families in Portland being tested and monitored? Is there a body at large who follows what happens to those that receive the treatments? Alters the composition of the injections, ever so slightly, each time they don't have the desired effect?

"This is crazy," Barnie finally says. "Completely crazy. You're trying to tell me the Yates tribe are a bunch of crazies because Henry Yates took some kind of mad scientist's formula?"

Arnold barks laughter. "Not at all."

"Then what?"

"I'm telling you we're crazy because *we* took the formula, Detective. It was administered to me. It was given to Rachel, Delilah, Daphne, Noland—we've all had it. Every damn one of us that remained in Portland since Henry Yates worked with Dr. Hawthorne."

He physically recoils, pushing the chair back and grabbing at his waist, as if to make sure his pistol is still in the holster.

"I'm harmless," Arnold says, smiling with his teeth. "Never hurt a fly. It seems that they've been working on that serum since the 19th century, Detective. Looks like most of the time it doesn't do much harm."

He stammers a curious reply. "They?"

Arnold puts the diary in his bag, ignoring the detectives suspicious flinch, and stands up. "That's the point I'm getting at. You want to investigate Rachel? Go right ahead. But you're barking up the wrong tree, if you ask me. If you really care about this violence in Portland. If you really care about what's made this city sick. If you want to right this wrong. Don't go looking at a pawn. Look for the King."

"You're not saying—"

"There's other families out there getting these injections," he declares. "And somewhere in Portland, there's a rotten underbelly working to study them and perfect it."

"But why?" Barnie asks, horrified. "*For God's sake*, why?"

He doesn't have a good answer to that question. "I don't know. But if you care about this city, I suggest you find out."

Death Lies There by Anna Vaks

Lone Fir

J ack walked into the Lone Fir Cemetery just a while past midnight with a rusted, worn-out shovel slung over his shoulder and a hatchet on his hip. As a rambling man, these possessions were a few of just a few more—he barely owned more than what he had with him just then. It was a moonless night, and cloudy, with rain forecasted to fall just about when he needed it to.

This time of year, far north as Oregon, no one would be walking about or awake so late, anyhow. It was cold enough to see his breath, and dark enough that once he walked through the pedestrian entrance and let the gate swing behind him, he couldn't see the street when he looked back.

Lone Fir was different than most of the small town cemeteries he'd hit before behind churches or monuments. For one, it was considerably older, built sometime in the mid 1800's. He could feel that age around him, and he didn't much like the way it sat on his shoulders. He was alone, but walking along the center path with barely a sound in the world, surprising since the city surrounded him. As his feet crunched on the frosty ground, he felt like he was being watched. Not even by a lone person, but by a stadium of people, all staring angrily at the man in the cemetery with a shovel slung over his back. What would a man walking along in a cemetery in the middle of a night with a shovel be up to, if not no good?

He wasn't a superstitious man. Far from it. Cemeteries meant nothing to him; neither did churches or monuments or heritage sites. Just places to make people who were lucky enough not to be dead feel better about people that were dead. Not monuments to the dead, but monuments to the colossal egos and arrogance of the living. He normally felt offended by them if they were big.

And Lone Fir was big. There had to be 25,000 to 30,000 people buried in the groves around him. If the cemetery wasn't a couple miles wide, then he wasn't six feet tall. The trees rustled in a stormy wind as he walked deeper into the stately park, headstones rising like rows of corn back home in Iowa on either side of him.

A big oak that had to be a couple hundred years old, bigger around than a Honda Civic, marked the Heritage Rose Garden. He peered at it for a moment, trying to master that odd paranoia that occasionally crept up on him in cemeteries, that he wasn't alone and that the dead men and women didn't appreciate his being there.

He disguised his attempt to gather his nerves by inspecting the tree. And he did inspect the tree—Jack Edding wasn't a liar. But he was mainly trying to get his heart to sit still and get his dumb runaway mind to settle down. He waited a few more minutes, and when the feeling only grew, he continued angrily on and deeper along the wooded path.

A few minutes past the big oak that marked the Heritage Rose Garden was the Soldiers Monument. He didn't have many morals, but even Jack Edding wouldn't rob a soldier's grave. No sir. Not unless he thought there was really something good in there. And normally, men brave and dumb enough to sign up to die for their country didn't have much money back home, or else, he figured, they wouldn't have signed up in the first place.

Really, the best things he could hope for in any grave was bits of jewelry or watches. If he could have only been alive back when the pharaohs were dying, he thinks he'd have been about the happiest damn man on Earth. Imagine a king that died and then brought a billion dollars into his casket with him, just waiting to be taken. Those old days he would have been a king himself after just a few years of digging up graves.

In the 21st century, the best he can hope for is some old jerk to kick the bucket and get buried with his favorite Rolex. He checks over old obituaries and looks for the long ones that seem like they were written by an estate. About a month ago he tracked down an old oil tycoon's plot and had a damn field day. Just a couple weeks after the old bag had been put in the ground, he walked into the Texas State Cemetery with the same shovel he had now and dug the old rotter up. Soil was still soft. Didn't even stink very much, considering how long he'd been in the ground. Modern day burials being what they are, sometimes he could pull open a casket that'd been planted a year or two earlier and not even be that grossed out. Cracked the oak casket with his hatchet, and found a $10,000 watch on each wrist, not to mention size 13 loafers that fetched him a couple hundred dollars.

It's not always that way, of course. Lots of times, he doesn't find much of anything. It's a lot of work to dig up a grave by hand. Six feet of earth doesn't get moved easy. Takes two or three hours just to hit the casket, and another twenty or thirty minutes to get in there depending on what it's made of. Then there's the part of his heart that'd ache not getting to walk through the lonely places at night and be by himself and yet not really be by himself, not ever, not in a cemetery.

That night in Lone Fir, he had that feeling more than ever before. He was alone in the big expanse. But he was also walking along with 10,000 men on his left and 10,000 women on his right and probably thousands of poor kids, too, that never got to grow up to be men or women and instead got buried here. He tried not to dig up kids, but some nights, like tonight, he was going in blind and it couldn't always be avoided. Normally kids aren't buried with anything worth much. Also, it just didn't quite feel right. Like the bit with the soldiers. Jack had morals. But he was just smart enough to know that sometimes a moral was worth stomping on.

He had a general idea of where he was going. Mainly, deeper into the cemetery. If at all possible, it was best to go into a corner. There wasn't a wall in the world Jack Edding couldn't, or wouldn't, climb over if he were pressed. If security came nosing around, normally, you could just lie down flat on the ground and they'd wander by on the predictable path they took. He found out a long time ago that security guards weren't actually looking for people. They were just walking and hoping not to see anything. They wanted to get back to their shack and catch up on whatever show or dirty story they'd picked out for that night's shift, just about as much as he wanted them to get the hell out of his way.

A cast of leaves fell from an old elm and they skittered across his path like a thousand tarantulas. The thought of all those leaves being spiders, the thought of those spiders scrambling madly toward him, made him get goosebumps all over his whole body. He took the shovel off his shoulder and thrust it angrily at the leaves and glared into the dark sky. What was the Big Guy playing at, trying to scare him like that? He didn't even believe in the Big Guy, and hated himself for thinking like that. But he found whenever he got scared that he was a damn sight more religious than when he was feeling safe and sound.

'Cause the Big Guy wouldn't be cool with people crawling up out of their graves, would he? The Big Guy wouldn't want an old convict or crazy, lunatic soldier driven mad by the war to animate his undead body, to punch his way out of his old pulpy casket that'd been torn apart by worms, and claw his way up and out of the ground. The Big Guy wouldn't want an army of dead or horde of ghosts to come...

He kept on, still feeling like Lone Fir was an awful name for a cemetery that felt so damn *full*. A tip from one of his buddies, a fellow capital GR Grave Robber, (who was getting so old these days that Jack thought he'd probably have to stop soon, or else die in one of the graves he was digging up from a heart attack) was another reason he thought going far into the cemetery might be worthwhile.

Portland being what it was back in the old days, there were some unscrupulous unmarked graves in Lone Fir for the undesirables that died in the late 1800s. Mental patients and immigrant workers, mostly. Jack wasn't sure if he fully believed his friend. He'd told him more than one tall tale before (like that he'd seen the ghosts of dead men, or that he'd seen footprints in the early morning dewy grass that began just before a headstone and ended right at the base of a brick wall, or that he once dug up a grave marked 1877-1922 and heard its inhabitant scratching helplessly inside)—but this one, about the unmarked graves, seemed like it could prove true.

'Course, you wouldn't think there'd be anything too neat in the grave of a man or woman so unimportant they didn't even get a marking on their stone. At least not if you only thought about it for a moment. But being a history major (and why do you think he was robbing graves now, if not because he was a history major) Jack knew that there was often a secret among immigrants in the late 1800s, particularly those in Oregon. They didn't much trust money, and to get to the United States, they often had to pay just about everything they had back home. Unless they hid it—and the only things small enough to hide were jewelry and bits of gold. Sometimes in a fake tooth, concealed for an emergency. Sometimes a coin kept in the old universal coin purse—he didn't like checking for that, but Jack always figured the old dead people didn't mind. It's not like he got off on it. No sir.

He figured as long as he didn't enjoy himself, it wasn't wrong in that way. And they were dead. He always felt he had to remind that little inner voice that talked to him accusingly of that. The damn people were dead and they didn't mind. Maybe they had some earrings or a ring or some gold teeth that'd last a hell of a lot longer than the white ones. Maybe they had an old pocket watch. Even crazies locked up in the mental asylum were known to keep things like that.

He padded along without even trying to be quiet, letting Lone Fir swallow him up with the tens of thousands of others it'd consumed over the centuries. He whistled a tune quietly, just for himself, and smiled up at the sky when it started to rain. Just in time. The light pitter-patter of the shower would help to muffle the sound of his shovel digging into the soft earth and piling up a six foot mound of dirt over his shoulder. Indeed, it made digging easier, too. Rain showers were one of his closest friends.

A great cap of moss crept up the top of a terrible willow, and Jack thought he could hear something crawling under it. An awful thought, and one he wished he'd never let slip into his head. *Just the damn wind*, he told himself, not quite believing it one way or another. A great stand of Eastern White pines caught his eye, and beyond them, some White oaks and Giant sequoias that seemed not to belong in Portland at all but had somehow thrived among all the dead things.

He thought, suddenly, of a bit of old Oregon folklore that he didn't even know he remembered up until the moment it leapt into his unsuspecting mind and assaulted him with its existence. Somewhere in this cemetery, an axe murderess named Charity Lamb was said to be buried. Like it or not, she was probably hidden along with all the other so called deplorables, with the immigrants and insane asylum folks dreaming their eternal slumber around her. He thought he could remember that she spent some time in prison before being transferred to Hawthorne's Insane Asylum in southeast Portland.

He was good and wet by the time he hit the back of the cemetery, and more than a little spooked at all the curious sounds that seemed to come from between the stones and radiate from behind the trees. There were Douglas firs and maples, some incense cedars that had to be well over a hundred feet tall and damn near looked like they stretched straight into the heavens, sprawling beech trees and gnarled, fissured black locusts that seemed like they were created just to stand watch over graves. Between them and around them were a thousand graves a minute, headstones peeking out of the green soil surreptitiously, all that remained to mark a whole life.

But there weren't any markers to commemorate the dead that'd been pushed into the far corner of the cemetery and covered up as if to save the world from having to remember them. He thought that was a bit wrong, and wondered that some social justice group or another hadn't hollered and shouted about it enough to get something done. It'd have helped him a bit to know exactly where to start digging.

But he didn't need it to be easy. Just fun. And digging was fine, even in a cemetery such as this, that seemed to feel him in its midst and hate him for invading it. He walked off the path and through the damp grass, feeling the way the dirt moved under his feet and trying to decide exactly where to go.

Finally, he dropped his shovel into the earth just a few paces away from an ancient eucalyptus, walking hard onto the step to drive it deep.

The earth seemed to sing as he pulled the first, crisp load of dirt free and tossed it over his back. Either that, or scream, and Jack wasn't much for worrying about which. It made him feel good to dig in the cemetery, it made him feel happy. He was a treasure hunter. And this here, why, he thought perhaps he wasn't even committing a felony. There wasn't a marked grave beneath his feet, no. Just the rumors of Portland's seedy, dark past to indicate that he might be digging up something that no one wanted him to find. And he could hardly be blamed for a city not having proper records or markers to signal where they'd put their dead, could he? Perhaps he was a madman that had a compulsion to dig and had purposefully wondered over here away from all the tombstones so that he wouldn't do anything wrong.

And don't ask questions about his hatchet, thank you very much.

A cusp of wind screamed through the woods and something like a shriek seemed to float on its back. Jack resisted the urge to turn and check over his shoulder, because doing that would be admitting that the superstition had worked its way into him and made him believe in things that couldn't be true. It'd also break the beautiful sheen that had begun to work into his mind.

He kept digging, suppressing the chills that rolled on his neck, working hard enough to build up a sweat. The ground seemed to want him to pull it up. An idea sprang into his head and he grabbed onto it, digging faster still, that the men and women buried unsanctimoniously here perhaps wanted him to know the secret and reveal it.

He had something else with him for that, something he always brought but had very rarely used. A high quality Polaroid that his father gave him sometime in the late 90s when he was just a kid. He could record what he found that way, and perhaps even if he didn't find a tangible treasure, he'd come away with proof that something odd had once happened here, something unscrupulous, something that ought to be rectified.

He was a couple feet deep when he heard footsteps. They were clear and steady enough to break him out of the digging trance, the high he chased from city to city like a junkie, perhaps the sole and solitary reason he was a grave robber in the first place. It wasn't an easy trance to break. It wasn't a simple high to come down from. Snapping out of it, suddenly like that, felt like someone had punched him hard in the gut.

He whipped around, swinging his shovel violently—

Only there was no one there. He scanned the darkness fearfully, breathing heavy out of his mouth. His heart thumped unevenly in his chest. A tree branch waved. Leaves scuttled across the ground.

Jack turned full around in a circle, moving fast and scanning desperately. Then he turned again, this time slow and careful. Nothing at all was moving in the Lone Fir cemetery. He was perhaps the only man at this end of Portland dumb enough not to be holed up inside, except for the ever increasing homeless population that had far better spots to hang out than this.

He was alone.

The digging high called to him, and like the addict he was, he turned and leaned back into the steadily deepening hole. He made it wider for a bit, recognizing there was no clear way to know he was aiming for a body (but also knowing that if thousands of unwanted bodies had been buried here that he could hardly miss). Then he started deeper.

It seemed the moment the glorious sheen came back over his vision that the paranoid thoughts faded and he let his primal self take over and perform work, like men used to do in the glory days, back before the industrial revolution robbed them of their ability to be the sole machines capable of creating complex things. He drove his shovel into the rapidly descending hole. He was well past his waist, getting deeper, when the clear and unmistakable sound of dragging feet broke him out of the clarity.

He popped his head up and climbed out of the hole fast as a mole, scrambling on his hands and knees in the wet, now muddy, grass. He spun about faster than before, panting like a dog that just chased a squirrel clear across a field. The rain came down faster now, and he was fully drenched in sweat and wet. He didn't care, though.

He scanned for the culprit of the noise.

He turned clear around once, fast, then again, slow. He wielded his shovel no longer like a tool but like a weapon. Someone was trying to sneak up on him. He'd heard the sound twice. He was certain what he heard. Positive. Jack knew what he saw and knew what he heard and knew what he said. No one could tell him otherwise.

Yet... beside the steadily falling rain and the dancing branches with their fluttering leaves and the 30,000 corpses around him, he was alone.

He called out in spite of what his eyes told him. "Hello? Who's there?" His voice was shaky and exhausted.

No one answered.

Jack looked into the hole angrily. He wasn't far from the right depth. He'd already done well over half the work. And—he checked over his shoulder again, turning full around to confirm—there was no one in sight.

Still. He heard the feet dragging. Clear as he could hear his shovel piling earth up behind him. Clear as he could hear the sound of his spade burying itself as he stepped on the hilt.

Anyone could be lurking behind one of the many trees around him. He'd look like a cat chasing a mouse if he were to try and check around all of them.

He ran a hand over his head to swipe the rain out of his wet hair and cursed angrily. "Got a hatchet on my belt," he called as he climbed back down into the hole furiously. "I'll use it. Don't want no trouble. I'm doing research, taking pictures for the press. I'm a reporter." He added this last bit almost as an afterthought.

The digging high came back. The sheen dropped over his vision. He deepened the hole, widened the hole, and suddenly—

Thwack. He hit soft pine, rotten in the dirt, thin and eaten up by worms and parasites. He'd felt the cut of pine like that a dozen times, at least. It's the kind they used for poor folk. The box had probably already been filled with dirt and the body inside it would be nothing but old bone with eaten up, rotten clothes atop it.

A big layer of dirt and splintered wood flew as he uncovered the coffin. When it was clear enough to see a big gash in the top, he leaned down and scraped at the ruined wood with a wet, bare hand, and recoiled sharply as something inside the casket moved.

He cursed, hesitating, grabbing at his hatchet to cut the snake or big worm or whatever the hell else might be living in that damp and putrid place in half when a scrambling, white hand shot out of the hole and grabbed at his wrist.

Jack thought screaming was for girls, but he let a frightened holler loose anyway. The hand was wet and cold, impossibly strong, and clean as a whistle. There wasn't a scrap of ligament or flesh or muscle on it. Jutting out of the tomb as it was, grabbing hard at his wrist, he could see the whole forearm and elbow was the same.

Nothing but bare, glistening bone.

Jack tried to pull his arm free and found the skeletal grip was somehow stronger than all the gas he had left in his tank. He swung his hatchet at it when twisting away didn't work, eyes bugging out of his head madly, screaming.

The bone broke like old driftwood; the anchor tying him four feet down in the dirty hole let go. He scrambled up, up, up, kicking dirt like an old dog that was covering up a bone, still screaming. His breath came in wheezing, whistling gasps, his lungs were pumping like the bellows in an old smithy, his legs barely worked.

The thing in the rotten casket scrambled and scratched, pushing dirt away. He heard it cracking upward, moving—

He tossed his hatchet up onto level ground, threw his shovel after it, and pulled himself out of the hole all in the span of a second. At any moment he was ready to kick his leg, his ankle, his foot, his toes, free. But nothing grabbed him to pull him back into the grave.

He was out. He splayed his hands out madly in the freshly muddy and wet earth around the hole and landed miraculously on the hilt of his hatchet, then on the handle of his shovel. He crawled blindly, blinking the rain and muck from his eyes, mumbling insanely.

The clear sound of feet walking broke from behind him and he twisted around on his back, screaming louder and higher than before, as the figure that belonged to that lumbering gait loomed over him and leered a broken, machine grin.

Distantly, in the way a man standing before a barreling train might notice an asteroid a thousand miles above his head, jetting right at him (and yet not so quick that the train wouldn't surely kill him first) he noticed that the now handless skeleton was crawling out of the grave he'd dug, just a few paces from him.

But before that, standing threateningly over him, was a rotten corpse with a toothless, sneering grimace and a large axe. The skin of the corpse's forehead was sloughing and wet, yet somehow alive. It was yellow and leaking pus; the eyes were full of maggots and moving madly with an insectile frenzy. The nose was a single stick of gristle that jutted from a raw and red channel that ran straight through to a jellied brain.

Blind, hot fear ran down his leg. Jack lost control of his bowels; he lost control of his whole body, and found that he couldn't take in a breath even as his lungs screamed at him to *work, dammit, work*. His hands fell loosely beside him and the sanity, the precious sanity he'd worked so hard for decades to build up, the ration and logic that all his reading and education built in him, ran wet and hot like so much piss from his unraveling mind.

The decaying corpse hefted the axe and something like a cackle came from its gashed throat as it swung.

Jack had just enough time to snap a single picture as the rain came down around him and the gleaming, rusted axe split his forehead like a dry log.

The Realization *by Igor Beltrame*

Asylum Avenue

Maria thought it was funny how tourists flocked to Hawthorne street, considering how not a damn one of them would want anything to do with someone that was truly crazy. And Hawthorne Street, which used to be known as Asylum Avenue, had a lunatic history.

She knew this because *she* was truly crazy—or at least she could be, on bad days, when her brain wasn't up to dealing with things. On days like that, she could be plum dangerous to be around. She knew it, and would tell it freely to anyone that spent enough time around her for it to matter.

"Pretty soon," she normally said, conversationally, "I'll probably go a little crazy again. You just steer clear of me, and then come back when I'm smiling again."

Most of the time, they didn't come back. The crazy bouts made keeping a good place to lie her head down hard, and holding a job even harder. More times than not, if the shelters were full up—and sometimes, she didn't even bother with the shelters on account of how dangerous it could be when it was time to leave and the *Black Van Men* would be parked on the opposite street looking for someone vulnerable to snatch—she'd just put up her tiny tent in a corner at the park.

It was getting cold, though, and in Portland, even the nice Salvation Army Surplus sleeping bags couldn't keep you warm when the snow decided it was going to fall. Last night the thin walls of her tent—more than a couple holes in those worn walls, more than a couple—were rattling and vibrating in the icy wind so hard they kept her awake. *Black Van Men* be damned, by 3 in the morning, Maria decided she'd be seeking out the warmth of a shelter for tomorrow night.

At daylight, she packed up, hiding her tent in the culvert ditch where she'd hid it for the last two years, and began the day the same way she began every day. Hoofing it over to the corner of 3rd avenue and shaking her cup for change. This was one of the safe places. Normally, within an hour, she could get enough for a cup of coffee and an egg sandwich. Today, she did—first from a little Black boy that asked his momma if they had anything to spare, then from an older white woman, and finally $2 from a man in a suit that was talking on the phone and didn't even spare her a glance. Like he was depositing the money into a homeless fund. He didn't care what she looked like.

But Maria didn't care that he didn't care. She pocketed the money, smiling toothlessly, and marched down the street to get her breakfast. It was near 10 by then, according to the clock outside Columbia Bank, and that was good because most of the chill had already been worked out of the air by the sun.

She saw Floyd at the sandwich shop, sitting outside the door with his back to the wall, munching on a ham and cheese with a cup of something hot between his legs. He used to be a jazz musician, back in the 80s, and with his untamed afro and scuffed leather boots, he still somehow looked the part—even if he hadn't strummed a bass guitar or played the trumpet for over 20 years.

"Maria!" he roared jovially when he saw her. "How's it hanging, pretty lady?"

Maria wasn't pretty, and she knew it. She hadn't been pretty since she was 40. Back then, when she was angry about it, she'd have been annoyed at the accusation. But now, with over a decade to get used to it, it made her feel good.

She told Floyd that she had enough for an egg sandwich and some coffee, and that she'd be out in a minute. The young man at the counter peered at her suspiciously when she made her order. Being inside the shop—being inside any building, even the shelter—made her feel a bit like she was an animal under surveillance at some kind of low tech zoo. She always wanted to get back outside as soon as she could.

He told her the price: $6.33, and looked surprised when she actually pulled it out. She paid for over half in quarters, counting them carefully, one by one. The television over the boys head was babbling about some kind of pandemic, and Maria shouted at it.

"Don't you know those things cause cancer?"

Someone in the back of the shop told her to shut up.

She turned, ready to fight—but no one was there. "Good riddance," she muttered.

Outside, almost warm in the winter sun, she sat with Floyd and enjoyed the breakfast, eating as slow as she could so that it would make her feel fuller.

"Was cold last night," the old musician said.

"Not as cold as that Christmas a couple years ago."

He grinned. Floyd still had perfect teeth, even though she knew he didn't own a toothbrush. Congratulations on the good genetics, Floyd. "You sleep out in the park?"

Only a few people in Portland knew where she slept. She looked around warily before answering. The only people on the street looked like tourists, and they weren't near enough to hear her admit it. "That's right. Was thinking of maybe going to a shelter tonight."

He whistled. "Dangerous."

Floyd knew about the *Black Van Men*, and had even scared them off before. He was one of the only good ones around these days, it seemed. Even though he was old, he was big, and tough. "Those folk would never want anything to do with an old dried up thing like me."

He raised his brows. "You're not so dried up as you seem to think, Miss Thang."

She took a drink of her coffee. "Well I was cold as a witches tit last night. I guess I'll just risk it." She looked at him sidelong, "unless you want to come with?"

Floyd considered. He mainly liked to stay out of shelters, although for different reasons than her. Women had to fear the *Black Van Men* because of sex trafficking and raping. Men like Floyd didn't have to worry about that. They just had to worry about younger, bigger or meaner guys trying to get in their business or step up on them. Being homeless in Portland was a bit like being a wolf. You had to mark your territory, and guard it—and if someone stepped into your lane, you either had to fight or run.

"I'll keep you safe," she joked. "We'll tell em' we're married, like we did in the old days. Remember that?"

He laughed. When Floyd laughed, even rich tourists, who normally only offered grimaces or averted eyes, would smile. "They'd never let me in come holiday if it wasn't for you. If you an old, Black man in this city and the shelters filling up, they'd rather let you die than give you a corner to lie your head in. Ain't that the truth?"

"Make it easier for those *Black Van Men* to prey on the women. Keep good men like you away and what will we do?"

"That's the truth." He leaned in conspiratorially, and she could smell the black coffee on his breath. "You want to know what I heard?"

She didn't like when people got close to her. Especially not if they had coffee breath. But she made an exception for Floyd. "What?"

"They post up out there at Hawthorne Street, where all them tourists like to go to look at the old buildings."

Her coffee was cool enough to drink, then, so she took a sip. She'd seen them on Hawthorne a few times. "Post up to do what?"

"Yank little kids, mostly. You know how many kids go missing in this city?"

She nodded. "I heard they worked for the Government. Mk-Ultra, mind control, you name it. I could tell you stories about Hawthorne Asylum that'd—" she shivered for effect "—make you curl up and cry!"

"Hawthorne Asylum been gone a long time," he batted back, "but them *Black Van Men* are here today."

She nodded. "I think they took that little old gal that used to run around here, what was her name?"

He frowned. "The white gal with the red hair, got kicked out her folks place for being one of those letters in the LGB-something-something?"

"That's right." The girls name was Alice, and Maria remembered her so well because she'd warned her not to hang out outside the shelters for too long, and not to talk to any men in black vans, and the dumb bitch had gone right up to one of the vans one day, like a kid trying to get some candy. She'd talked to one of the *Black Van Men* and, next thing you knew, *jumped right in the van with them*. She recounted the story to Floyd, and he was shaking his head sadly before she was half finished.

"You can't even lead some of these young ones to water, let alone make them drink! It's a sad world."

For a while, she didn't say anything. Sometimes it felt like Floyd knew what she was thinking. They were on the same wavelength. If they were radios, they'd be playing the same music. Maybe her station would be a little louder, and the disc jokey would tell funny stories between tracks. Maybe his would talk about politics and give an hourly traffic update. But they'd be playing the same songs, by mainly old school Black artists, and they'd never let any major corporation advertise their bullshit snake oil between the hour, either. No way.

They spent the rest of the day wandering around Portland together, shaking their cups when they thought someone might be cajoled into dropping a dollar inside. Floyd did better than her, collecting $7.80, compared to her $6.50. He normally beat her during the wintertime, when there were less tourists. Somehow the locals trusted him more, even though she'd been around a bit longer and liked to wear shirts that said *Portland* on them. It was easier to get a lot more than $7.80 or $6.50 in Portland—but they didn't like to be pushy or go to the most congested areas. It was safer to hang out in the low pop places, with gentler people.

They ate at a food truck for dinner, a couple of tacos each for $2.50 —the cheapest in Portland, or maybe even all of Oregon, and they weren't stingy, neither. You could get a whole corn tortilla stuffed with beans, cheese, chicken, cilantro, lime, onion, and tomato, with a little drizzle of sour cream on top, *times two*, for less than three bucks. Who could beat it? Floyd washed it down with a bottle of cola, onc of the old machines tucked away into a nearly forgotten corner, you could get one for 75 cents when most others were nearly twice that. She had water.

They cut through the High School field adjacent to the park about an hour before sundown, not rushing.

"Place is built on an old volcano," Floyd said.

She looked at him carefully, trying to see if he was playing with her. "For real?"

"Deadly serious," he said, "serious as that virus all the rich people seem to keep getting."

She cawed laughter at that. Rich folk seemed to get sick a lot more than poor. "Where's it at?"

He wrinkled his nose. "Where's what?"

"The volcano," she grinned.

"Oh, that?" He shrugged, like he'd already almost forgot about it. "I guess it's under our feet. They said it's an old one, don't work anymore."

"Seems like most volcanoes are tired of making smoke these days." She thought that might be a metaphor for something else, but couldn't quite make it stretch. She wasn't good at metaphors, or similes, or any of that other English crap.

They drew up to a big pool in the center of the park with a little sign that named it *City of Portland Reservoir Number 5*. The water was still. A scattering of stale oak leaves skidded across the surface, like little ships with no sails. On the other side of the pool, a twin pair of red cedars stood like sentinels. Floyd walked up nearly to the waters edge and took a big breath. She thought he looked like someone trying to take a drink of air.

He looked back at her. "You hear old Johnny Bigwalker got out of prison?"

She scowled. She hadn't heard anyone say that redneck bastards name in years. He came from Arkansas sometime in the early 2000s, joining the homeless population and making waves just about the moment he showed up. He sold drugs and pimped vulnerable girls. Maria knew for a fact he'd give anyone—man or woman—a $10 bill if they were willing to give him a sexual favor. She'd never been desperate enough to take him up on the offer. He was a gross guy. And she'd never sold sex, not even when she was crazy.

"Got bad memories of him?"

"Thought he went away for good is all."

"Got out due to overpopulation," Floyd said, shaking his head to show he thought that was a load of bullshit. "Imagine killing a man and then getting to walk free 'cause they don't got room to keep you locked up."

"That's just the one he got caught for." Maria was nearly certain Johnny Bigwalker was to blame for more than a couple disappearances between 2004 and 2008. He ran with a bad crowd, just about the worst of the worst. Lots of them were still around, today. But Maria knew where they liked to operate—she had their number, yessir—and she steered real clear of them. Just like the *Black Van Men.*

"I guess he'll be back to doing no good soon enough." He sighed heavily and clapped a hand on her shoulder. It made her feel like a little girl again. Floyd reminded her of her Grandpapa. "Anyway, just thought you should know."

She let his hand sit there longer than she would anyone else, and then shrugged it off. "Thanks for the warning. You ready to go?"

By the time they got to the shelter, it was good and dark. They had a couple of beds open, and like it or not, Floyd probably wouldn't have gotten one on his own. But Maria vouched for him, going over the top to sell it so the college educated white girl that manned the desk would believe them. She called him Sweety and even put her arm through his.

She and Floyd saw a couple people they knew there, and got to talking with them about Johnny Bigwalker, and other unfortunate members of their homeless community that they all rather wished would just blow away in a sharp wind. They talked about the *Black Van Men, too,* and promised they'd watch out for one another.

Maria slept well that night, and was warm until 7 AM., when dawn came and started to light the room. She left the shelter with Floyd, a pair of younger girls that looked alike enough to be twins but had been born on opposite sides of the country, and a young boy that couldn't have been old enough to get a beer down at the pub.

The black vans, four panels with no plates, were parked at the end of the street. Maria stepped into the morning sunlight and spotted them almost immediately, and pointed them out to the others. "But don't all look at once," she said. Of course, everyone did.

"I'd be careful if I were you, girls," Floyd said.

They didn't seem certain that the black vans were actually anything to fear. Hadn't been around Portland long enough, maybe, or just young and dumb. Maria found that the younger you were, the less you thought anyone would hurt you, and the less you believed that people were out to get you. Which was funny, because the younger you were, the better you were to those kinds of freaks. By the time you got old enough to realize what was going on—if you were lucky enough to get old, that is—they mostly didn't want to mess with you.

Maria tried to convince them when she saw their doubtful expressions. "I've seen them take girls just like you."

They promised to be careful—but she got the distinct feeling it was more lip service than anything genuine. They didn't perceive those seemingly empty vans as threats. But she'd seen them pull up outside the shelter a hundred times before, an hour or two before sunrise. And she'd seen them pull away, too, floating listlessly down the street after a young and vulnerable homeless person, seemingly just going for a cruise. She'd tried to follow, once, but she got an asthma attack before she'd gone half a block. Asthma without an inhaler is serious business. She'd given up on it after that.

They watched the girls go.

Floyd crossed his arms. "Got any plans?"

She didn't, aside from finding something to eat. She thought she might go to her normal place, by the doughnut shop, with all the tourists. "Just same old. Want to come back and sleep here tonight? I'll vouch for you."

He thought about it, and then shook his head. "Was thinking about sleeping in the park again. I don't like those walls. Make me feel like I might get stuck and never get out again. And..." he scratched the back of his head "...I don't know. Guess I feel like you're the only person I like around here."

She crinkled her brow. "That a bad thing?"

"Maybe feels like everyone I like, if I spend much time around them, ends up not liking me very much. Or I end up not liking them, maybe."

"Gotta keep me at arm's length?" She nodded, feeling again like they had a lot of the same thoughts. If she didn't get the crazies... if she could hold a job and was healthy in her head, maybe...

But she found entertaining those thoughts of being normal always led to the same place. Get her down in the blues, make her sad. It was best not to. She wasn't normal. She had bad thoughts, and a bad head, and medicine had never helped.

"I know what you mean. But don't be a stranger. I like to see you around, Floyd. Makes me feel good to know there's still good ones out here."

He promised she'd see him around more often. Said he'd stop for a sandwich tomorrow morning at their usual place. And then he left, around the same corner the girls had.

Maria never saw him again.

A couple of months later, long time after Maria had given up on finding out what happened to Floyd—after she'd asked everyone they knew, gone to all their usual haunts, talked to every shelter, every corner man, even some of the bad ones, she was walking through Mt. Tabor Park, wrapped up in a puffy Red Cross coat with her hands shoved deep into the pockets. It was deep winter now; there was a heavy crust of ice on the ground, and more scheduled to freeze over later. She'd been out of the shelter for a few days, sleeping in her tent and doing her best to stay warm. The nights were getting cold. Almost too cold.

She walked up to the same pool she and Floyd had stood at, what seemed like just a few days ago, but what must have been November. Now, in late February, the pond stood cold and still. The sign was still there to mark it: *City of Portland Reservoir, Number 5*. Dirty ice clung to the face of it. There weren't any late leaves skittering around anymore, or ripples brought about by the wind. It appeared as an unyielding mass. Maria thought she knew how it must feel to be frozen like that.

It was already getting dark, and the park was nearly deserted. But something kept her rooted to the spot. It was quiet. Portland loomed around the park. A few blocks away, someone laid on their horn, probably honking at someone in a cross walk. She took a deep breath. A window broke, somewhere closer.

Then the park lit up with the sound of a quiet engine. Maria turned, trying to find the source of it, not quite understanding. There were paths in the park, meant for golf carts and other small vehicles, but there wasn't a road fit for driving a big vehicle on.

Yet... there.

She saw it gliding through the shadows, tires spilling over on either side of the blacktop like a bear bumbling down a hallway. A black four panel van with no license plate.

Her heart flew into her throat. She looked around for someone—anyone—and came up empty. The van was coming gently toward her, screaming headlights flooding the dark and washing it away, nearly blinding her. The path was just a rock's toss away. They'd see her standing there alone in just a couple seconds.

She fell to her belly and crawled like a toddler toward the nearest tree. The van, meanwhile, kept piping along at a steady, lulling speed. It came just before her, and then drew even with her. She held her breath. Her asthma twitched and flared. Her lungs and throat threatened to revolt, warning her with a burning ache. She wanted to cough.

The van kept going. She saw a shape inside the drivers window, which was illegally tinted at least a few shades too dark. It sat perfectly still and didn't look to the side as it passed.

Her heart thundered and flopped like a fish that'd grounded itself after trying to jump upstream. She was safe. And yet not safe at the same time. The van was past. But why was it in the park in the first place?

Hadn't Floyd told her he'd seen the *Black Van Men* in the park before? Wasn't that right around the last time she'd ever seen him?

Maria stayed on her belly, nearly kissing the trunk of the cedar tree she'd fallen next to. It smelled dead because of how cold it was. But she could remember how it was supposed to smell. She imagined that underneath that frozen skin which kept its core warm enough to survive, if she were to hack into it, there'd still be that good cedar smell that'd make her head light and cause her to dream about when she was a girl and she lived on a pig farm in Oklahoma.

The van slowed, a good hundred yards away.

Something stirred on the path behind her, and she tensed up, ready to scream and run and holler and pull out her knife and wave it around like a crazy lady. Feeling like she was about to *become* a crazy lady. It'd been a while since she had a good bout of the wild brain. Maybe now was the perfect time.

A man was walking up the path, after the van. A tall man with a bright moon face and boots that *click, click, click,* clacked as he plowed down the trail, somehow louder than the van with the big engine under its hood and the four big wheels to crunch twigs and leaves.

If she could have melted into the ground, she would have. If she could have just became a big pile of mud and sank into the soil, if her fear could have transformed her, she'd have let it. She missed Floyd, suddenly, sharper and harder than she had in weeks. If only Floyd were here. If only Floyd were here, he'd know what to do and he'd be able to protect her.

But the man wasn't looking toward *City of Portland Reservoir Number 5*. He had eyes only for the van. She watched him approach, squinting through the dark, which was especially oppressive here in the park. The van's red taillights helped to light things up a bit. But still, it was hard to make out much about the man, other than his backpack and his boots and his bright face.

He passed her without ever knowing she was there, just a few feet away, lying in the dirt on her belly. His boots *clacked* on the pavement. His eyes looked forward, always, at the van.

It took Maria a moment to place him. When she did, her heart got colder, and more afraid, somehow, than it already was.

Johnny Bigwalker. It was Johnny Bigwalker, the murderer, the drug dealer, the rapist, the human trafficker, walking along in a deserted park a long time after sundown to meet up with one of the *Black Van Men*.

Maria sensed she was somewhere she wasn't supposed to be. That she was seeing something—and would soon see and hear more—that she was never supposed to see or hear. That realization made her afraid.

She wanted to run after he'd walked past. But she wasn't fast. And her asthma was working hard to cut off her air. Making it hard to even think, let alone get up and run. It was taking all her concentration just to keep quiet. She wanted to start gasping and hacking. Her lungs *needed* her to wheeze and cough. If she could just cough, she'd be able to breathe again. Her throat was protesting, too. Tightening up. Getting small and funny feeling.

The black van's engine quit idling and cut off. The driver opened the door, got out, stepped onto the ground, and swung it hard behind him.

Johnny Bigwalker met him, and they began to talk.

The *Black Van Man* had a briefcase pinned under a big, muscled arm. "You do the job?"

"Always do the job," Johnny Bigwalker answered smoothly. "You don't got to ask. I'm a man of my word."

"We need another. Man this time, middle aged at least."

Johnny Bigwalker crossed his arms. "Again? You know that black sonofabitch almost took my head off, last time. I need more if you're going—"

The *Black Van Man* interrupted him harshly, in a cold, steely voice. "You'll get more."

"Cause it's dangerous," Johnny Bigwalker pressed. "You want middle aged men instead of little kids and women. It's a different ballgame."

"Don't think a man like me realizes that? We can find someone else if you're not capable. Can you do the job, or not?"

Johnny Bigwalker bristled. "I can do the job."

Maria inched a little closer to try and see the pair better. She wasn't brave enough to do more than stick just the tip of her nose out past the tree. Johnny Bigwalker and the black van man were standing almost nose to nose. The black van man was slightly bigger than Johnny, but Johnny was thicker around the middle and seemed like he wasn't intimidated in the slightest. There was something to be said about a man who had nothing to lose. Not even a home. He was dangerous in the way that a wild animal was dangerous. Perhaps even more dangerous than an animal, because a man like Johnny Bigwalker wasn't even afraid of being hurt.

"Good." He pushed the briefcase to him. "You got what you need in there. For last week."

"And what about for next week?" Johnny sounded like he was complaining. "I need to eat. I got boys who need to eat."

"It's there."

He started to open it, and the black van man's hand shot out to grab his wrist. "Not here. You do that later."

Johnny shook the man's hand off roughly. "Fine."

The black van man turned, opened the door, and stepped back into the van without another word. It seemed to Maria like more than half the conversation had been left unsaid. Where would they meet, and when? Who, exactly, was he going to bring?

And what had he meant about *that black sonofabitch*?

Something stirred in Maria's belly the more she thought of that. So the black van men were going after grown men, too? And Johnny Bigwalker was helping them snatch people? Girls, children—she'd known about that for her whole life. But grown men? Middle aged or older?

She thought of Floyd and her heart ached at the thought...

Could Floyd have taken Johnny's head off? Damn right he could have. Could he have fought him in a fair fight and won? She thought so. But if Johnny had come up behind him, or had some friends, maybe even Floyd wouldn't have been able to fight.

The black van's engine rumbled to life in the middle of the park. The taillights blinked and stared like violent animals. Pointing the other direction, the headlights flooded the other end of the park in harsh yellow light. The black van man knocked it into gear and took off. Maria said a silent thanks to whoever was looking out for her— perhaps, she hoped and also didn't hope, Floyd himself—that the black van man didn't decide to turn around and come back this way to shine his lights on her again. Escaping notice once was plenty good.

Johnny watched as the van crawled through the park before finally disappearing behind a stand of pine trees. He stood still all the while, fiddling with the briefcase, tapping his boot on the hard ground.

Then he turned, coming back the way he entered, and Maria sank down behind the pine tree a little lower. Her mind was working overtime just to try and put things in order. She felt the crazies licking at the back of her skull like fire ants. They would bite into her, start to light her up and make her itch, and then suddenly she'd be *Manic Maria*, as her brother used to call her.

Her heart picked up speed again as she felt herself—or she felt part of herself, which she normally kept hidden, wake up. And suddenly Maria was picking herself up from behind the tree, not even trying to be quiet, and coming out from the shadows around the reservoir.

She stepped into the road and cut Johnny Bigwalker off. She'd expected him to jump back in surprise as she came out of the bushes, or at least act surprised or nervous.

He looked at her calmly and evenly instead, and came to a stop a good twenty paces away. "You been listening to us?"

She didn't deny it. "I think you're a bad man."

He put his thumbs in his waistband, like a guy from a cheesy, old movie. "Guilty as charged. You gonna arrest me, officer?"

He took a step closer and squinted at her. "Do I know you?"

"I know you," she said. Truth was, she wasn't sure if Johnny Bigwalker knew her, personally. Most people didn't—although they'd seen her around, maybe, she didn't favor many with her name or conversation. "And I know you did something bad to someone I care about. And I want you to admit it."

He crossed his arms. "I'm gonna give you about 5 seconds to get the hell out of my way. And if you aren't, I'm going to break your head on this pavement and nobody will ever know who did it."

The fire ants sank their little pincers into her brain, all at once, and her mind slipped markedly away from the sane reality it'd been immersed in for the last few months and into the deep zone she thought of as her *laughing place*.

"When did you take that black man you were talking about?"

He scoffed and started to come forward. "I'm not answering shit to you, crazy lady."

Maria clutched the knife in her pocket as he came. Her arm trembled. Johnny Bigwalker didn't seem afraid that she could, or would, defend herself. He didn't seem to have any thought at all, other than of killing her and then walking away, just like he said he would.

"Going to kill you," he said, almost like a prayer.

Maria pulled the knife fast out of her pocket, depressed the button, and plunged it hard into Johnny's bright moon face as he stepped forward and grabbed at her neck.

He screamed—roared, really—and that sound woke the whole park. His clutching hand didn't let go of her, although he doubled over and cringed away from the knife, which had stuck deep somewhere below his right eye.

He still had his hands on her. She wriggled and jigged like a wild cat, trying to shake free. He threw her hard on the ground—she took most of the weight on her hip, grunting at the pain, but she was free, now. She leapt back to her legs and growled at him, feeling the crazy coursing through her and no longer caring about it.

She still had her knife in her hand. Johnny was bleeding heavily out of his face. He brought a hand up and wiped his cheek. He screamed.

"When did you take that black man?" she asked again. "Did you know his name?"

He came at her again, lunging like a drunk man.

She swung—connected with the meaty palm of his hand, cutting deep—and he jolted back, howling like a hurt dog. One of his fingers flew off, cut completely clean, and Maria thanked her sane self for polishing and sharpening this little three inch blade, about half a year ago, when she'd found it on the sidewalk outside the County Library.

Johnny's coconut pie face transformed before her. Bleeding, heaving, overcome with malice. He screamed, and this time he didn't lunge. He charged.

Maria stabbed at him as he came. He drove himself into the knife, taking it hard in the chest, but he didn't fall back this time. There was too much of him coming forward. He wrapped her in his arms, falling on her, still screaming.

She screamed, too. But not because she was afraid. Cause Johnny was a big man, and he was coming down on top of her. Even though she'd stabbed him, he might have enough left in the tank to choke her.

His hands started to look for her throat. She left the knife buried in his chest and started fighting them off. He forced a bloody paw into her face and she bit it, not caring that he probably had diseases, just wanting to live to see the morning.

He howled again and punched her so hard, her head thudded into the pavement. She saw stars. Her vision faded a bit—and then came back as he drove a forearm into her throat and nearly cut off her air supply wholesale.

She had enough energy, and air, for one last attack. She drove her knee up, between Johnny's legs, and punched it hard into his groin.

The breath went out of him in a harsh *oof.* The pressure on her neck let up. She pushed Johnny off and he rolled over, landing on his back, gasping and wheezing. His face was soaked in blood, his hand was a red glove.

She grabbed the knife out of his chest, scrambling on her hands and knees to get on top of him, and his whole body convulsed harshly as she pulled it free.

She drove it into him again, aiming for his belly so he didn't die instantly, and he howled breathlessly.

Then she got to her feet.

He was still alive. Breathing shallowly. Glaring heatedly at her. The briefcase was now just a short toss away.

"When did you do it?" she asked for the third time. "You said you took a Black man. When?"

Johnny raised his good hand and flipped her off.

Maria dove at him, screaming, and stabbed him in the leg.

Once. Twice. Three times—and finally he was crying, "all right, all right!"

She stopped. Her asthma was acting up again. Her lungs were desperately close to giving up. She tried to hide it as best she could.

"Guess it wasn't long after I got out," he whispered bloodily. "November. Late November. Was a big man with an afro. Did you know him or something?"

Maria didn't speak. Her mind twisted and contorted. For an instant, she felt reality itself give way completely. She couldn't think or see.

"Leather boots," he added. "Nice ones. I sold them for twenty five dollars."

She felt herself coming back, just enough to think rationally. She looked at Johnny, trying to decide if he'd live. His eyes were getting glassy. He was bleeding heavily from four different places.

She weighed the risk and decided she'd be long gone from here pretty soon, anyway, and turned her back on Johnny for good. She was crying. She pressed the knife's button and put the blade back inside it, not even bothering to wipe it off. She'd have time for that later, maybe, when she came back to herself.

Johnny gurgled something at her as she went for the briefcase. She couldn't hear what he said, and didn't care.

She picked it up—running her hand over the smooth leather, and looked around carefully. It was lighter than she'd expected. They'd made a lot of noise. There were lots of people out in Portland after dark, even in the winter. But she didn't see anyone.

She opened the briefcase, thumbing hard at the latch with shaky hands, and laughed shortly as an assortment of things fell out. Rope, handcuffs, a hard clunk—that was a black gun, probably loaded—a big hunting knife.

And two wads of cash.

She ignored everything except for the cash, feeling sick as she picked them up. They were bands of 20 dollar bills, not so thick as they were in the movies.

Still. It was more money than she'd ever seen. By about—she thumbed the stack, and then brought it up to her face so she could read the little band—yes, by about $2000.

The assortment of items on the ground—the briefcase itself—would tell its own story to whoever found Johnny. She didn't want any of it.

Not even the gun. She had no use for a weapon like that.

She shoved the cash into her waistband, pulling her bloody, torn shirt over it, and turned back around to step around Johnny Bigwalker's shaking, bloody body. Off to find the first cabbie that'd take her out of Portland. She thought she'd go south, to California—somewhere warmer—and start a new life. She hoped there weren't *black van men* there.

Ulterior Motives by Roval Tarroza

Nazi Cop

They walked into Forest Park just a while past midnight, well after their shifts at the police department had ended and most of Portland had gone to sleep for the night. This was work best left for these quiet hours. The shrine wasn't the kind of thing that looked good in daylight. Karl thought it was something about the way history had shunned the symbols so totally, and so unfairly, that made them such a peculiar sight for the average person in the year of 2020.

The park, for its part, was inviting. It was cold out, and quiet; the trees shifted in the breeze and the branches reached and clawed hungrily. Sometimes it seemed like they were looking for something. Karl thought they were like blind men feeling around in their bedroom. The leaves fell off like little ants in the fall. The ants scurried and skittered through the park, looking for crumbs or feet or toes, whatever leaf-ants ate.

Robbie and Laz were with him tonight. Robbie had been worshiping at the shrine for years, and he could attest to the benefits the old power was capable of bestowing on someone willing to kneel before it. Not that Karl needed anyone to attest to anything. Just about every good thing that ever happened to him was thanks to whatever old power had come gliding into Portland around the turn of the 21st century. He'd been working like a dog to keep it there ever since, doing what little things a man of his status could to keep a big thing like that in place. It was like a mouse trying to chain down a lion.

Laz was relatively new. He'd been out to the shrine with them a few times. Initiating a new guy could be dangerous, especially in the age of Twitter and cell phones and political correctness. It seemed to Karl like you could get fired these days just for telling someone you didn't have the same opinion as them. Pathetic. He felt bad for the guys who didn't have the power of the shrine. He'd been up to his neck in that shit before, once someone recorded him worshiping the power. It didn't look good with no context, frankly. Even with context, he knew a lot of limp wrist assholes wouldn't care that he was nurturing a God. They saw one thing—a little symbol which they didn't even understand—and went absolutely bonkers. Whatever. Let them. As the years passed, he felt himself becoming less and less interested in the opinions of the general public. He cared less and less about the people he hurt and the blood he spilled, too. It was all just fuel for the power.

They didn't talk while they walked deeper into the trees, because they weren't always the only guys out there, not even at midnight. That's something else altogether, though—the things going on in Forest Park—Karl didn't want to think about them. He cleaved to the power when things got too funky. Blinking lights in the sky, creatures crawling up out of holes, dead men getting up out of the ground. Gave him the heebie-jeebies. All that shit was unnatural, and confusing, and honestly a little scary. If it weren't for the power, he probably would have left Portland a long time ago, gone someplace like Alabama or Florida. It never occurred to him that things were weird in Portland, *because* of the power.

The power liked swastikas. He couldn't help that. People called him a Nazi—and he guessed he had to admit he had a lot in common with the Nazi's. Adolf knew about the power, Karl was certain about that. There was no question about it. And look at all he'd been able to do because of it. He'd mobilized an entire nation, pulled the whole damn world into a war. He really brought the wool out of the walls on that one. He damn near soaked up all the power he could, Karl figured. That's why the Germans were so powerful at first, the power was damn near frantic and hysterical with all the blood they were giving it. It could have lifted a mountain!

The best *he* could do was stir up some shit on a local level. The power liked pain and blood. Karl fed it the best he could, but he was nothing compared to the holocaust. Still, there was still some latent power from all those events floating about in the ether, there was still some pain and trauma that could be wielded to feed the power and make it swell and be useful.

"Just a little further," Laz said, as if he were the one leading them into the woods.

Karl didn't reply, and neither did Robbie. The two of them looked at each other. He could read the expression on Robbie's bemused face. Laz was a bit of a dunce, a bit of a moron. He came from Arkansas, if that didn't tell you all that you need to know. The guy was a grade A hick, a real classic hillbilly, a literal idiot. Still, he was good enough to get on the force, and that meant he was good enough to worship at the shrine.

And he was right, after all. A few minutes later, they came through a particularly dense thicket and into a little clearing. In the middle of the clearing there were the dark shapes just barely lit up by the crescent moon that seemed to channel the power in the way a lightning rod in a barren field could channel lightning during a thunderstorm. He'd mounted the metal swastika to a big Douglas Fir that he illegally cut down last summer. That's how long they'd been at this spot, just a bit over a year, and so far, so good.

Robbie breathed a sigh of relief as they stepped out of the trees and approached the metal symbol. It was shivering slightly in the cold air, as if it could feel the temperature and was being warmed by their approach. Laz started muttering quietly, perhaps to himself, perhaps to the power at large, or maybe to no one and nothing in particular. Karl, for his part, tried to tune them out. He tried to tune out the whole world.

He listened for the sound of the metal swastika thrumming in the wind. Sometimes, if things were just right, you could hear it ringing like a bell. He felt a swell of love in his heart for the symbol and all the things it represented as he came up to the base of it. If all the power in the world could be summed up in one feeling, this had to be the way an artist would represent the feeling of power. Thinking about all the tribulations in history which this thing was lurking beneath or overtop made his head go light and he started to feel funny.

"It's hungry," Robbie said meekly. He wasn't normally a meek man, but the power made even the bravest and most boisterous people quiet and careful.

"Can we feed it tonight?" Laz asked hopefully.

Karl thought about it. The power fed mainly off pain. There was a lot of ways to cause pain, of course, and a lot of times, the physical trauma of killing or hurting wasn't at all what the power liked to feed on. That'd be like eating nothing but chicken breast for the rest of your life. It's nutritious, and it could feed you, but without seasoning and different ways of cooking and adding in some sides, you might go crazy. Karl didn't want the power to go crazy. He figured that was the way the world would end—whenever people forgot about it and decided to stop feeding it because of some politically correct B.S., that's when things would really go to shit.

Hurting people on a spiritual level, now that's where things really got worthwhile. You had to make someone feel little to really get a good glut of blood into the air. That's what he specialized at. It was easiest to do it in the poor parts of town. Take one look at Hazelwood, or really any of east Portland, and you'd know exactly why. The poor saps who grew up in those shit holes were barely keeping their head above water most days. Homelessness, drug addiction, gangs, even just general crime like robbery and petty theft. It was the perfect hunting ground. He looked at those people—almost always minority, which the power seemed to especially appreciate—like livestock just waiting to feed his beast.

"Sure," he said. "We can feed it tonight. I thought we ought to stand around a while though and listen to it first. Let it know we're here, and watching. It likes to feel us, you know?"

The two of them nodded in general agreement. It was undeniable that the power could feel them there. They were a paltry audience compared to the drones of SS that used to stand and wave and cheer and celebrate. Nonetheless, they were there. He felt sometimes like he'd been born in the wrong generation, at the wrong time, in the wrong place. If he could have been around back then? If he could have stood among the droves of adoring members of the power's religion? If he could have just *heard* Adolf's voice?

The other boys felt the same, largely. He'd explained it all to them. It wasn't just the Nazi's, (who were entirely misunderstood, and yet somehow perfectly understood at the same time by historians around the world). It was nearly every great and aggressive military power throughout time. He'd studied it thoroughly, not with Google or something lame like that, but at the library, with real books, like a professor. There were telltale signs. The power always had to be fed. It was clear when it was involved in things.

The world had gotten dangerous though. Maybe Hitler just did it too well. Maybe he wielded the power too expertly, with too much authority. Maybe he was just better at it than he was supposed to be, or the technology had caught up and made the influence the power afforded someone too dangerous. But things had changed forever after that war, that's for sure. Things had changed so totally that most people seemed to think there never would be another war like that. Of course that would be a tragedy for the power—to see it wane and weaken and shrivel up rather than grow and spread out.

Race was the easiest button to press these days. They were burning down cities again over paltry shit like killing a criminal in the street rather than letting him suck down a generation of taxpayer dollars to have a bogus set of court hearings and then live in confinement where he'd do nothing but shit and eat and have gay sex for the rest of his miserable life. Not so long ago it would have been a public service to take care of a leech like that. It would have gotten him in real tight and nice with the boys in Germany. It would have made him something like a hero. He had the balls to do the hard thing, the thing no one wanted to admit had to be done. That's why the power had sought him out, near as he could tell. It was clear to anyone that looked at Karl that he was capable of killing and hurting.

"I wish we could do more," Laz whined after a few cold minutes had passed. "I get to feeling like—"

Robbie cut him off. "We're doing all we can! What do you know? You've only been here for a few months."

Laz bristled. "That's a load of shit! Maybe fresh eyes see clearer than cloudy old ones like yours. You've gotten soft on it. Can't you *tell* it needs more? Can't you—"

Karl dropped a big hand on Robbie's shoulder a second before he was going to haul back and crack Laz across the side of the head with a punch that very well might have knocked him clean out.

"He's not wrong," he said gently.

Robbie turned to him, chest heaving angrily. He was quick to get mad. That's what the power liked about him, Karl thought. All that rage was useful.

He looked hurt. "You think we haven't been doing good?"

"We've been trying," Karl allowed, just so he didn't fan the flame. "But we could try harder. I think I've got a plan. A good one."

"A good one?" Laz said interestedly, nearly oblivious to the fact that he'd nearly had his head taken halfway off his shoulders.

"Need to stoke those fires that've been flaring across the country," Karl said. He already knew the boys would find the idea to be good. Not just because it *was* good, but because they hated migrants and criminals and druggies as much as he did. It wasn't chance that all the scum of Portland lived in the same neighborhood. That's just how they were. Like a big troop of animals that found a home in a concrete jungle—it was their nature. The world would be better off without them, the world would have been better off if the Germans had been made able to finish what they'd started, and maybe if they'd expanded a few of their more lenient policies, maybe if—

Robbie clued him in to the fact that he'd fallen into thought. "What were you gonna say? Stoke what fires?"

"The *race* fires!" Karl interjected furiously. "The god damned race fires you dolt."

Laz had heard all he needed to. "Yes! Exactly, that's exactly what it needs. How are we going to do it?"

Robbie looked at him expectantly.

"You boys are going to kill a coon," Karl said coolly, "and I'm going to video tape it."

They looked at one another for a moment, then back to Karl.

Robbie asked, "you gonna show our faces?"

Karl glared at him. "Do you think the power would let you get caught or in trouble?" He turned on Laz, who had the decency to also be frowning at Robbie. "Do you?"

"Not me!" Laz protested. "I'll put my face on every Newspaper in the world if that's what you think we ought to do. Whatever Hitler needs—"

"It's not *Hitler*," Karl growled for the hundredth time. Laz was more fascinated with Nazi's than even he was, and he had this ridiculous notion that the power was Hitler himself.

"Fine," Laz relented. Sometimes he'd argue the point, but right now he was clearly too excited. "If *the power* wants us to do it, then we'll be able to do it. Right? It'll make sure it happens. Just like the holocaust, it was meant to happen, and so it did. It gave the Germans the power to do it. Right?"

It was starting to get cold out, and they'd had this conversation too many times. Laz was mostly correct about that part, anyway, so Karl just nodded. "Right." Then he fixed Robbie in his sternest, most thoughtful gaze. "Right?"

Robbie's mustached upper lip trembled a little. He had a peculiar look on his face, like he was being pulled in two different directions. His expression and attitude were both completely surprising to Karl, who thought he'd be willing to do anything that was asked of him without second thought.

Finally, he nodded his consent. "All right. Long as it's one that deserves it. A druggie or a gangbanger, or at least a homeless person. Okay? Not just some random Black, but a criminal."

"They're all guilty out in Hazelwood," Laz said happily. "All guilty of one thing or another. Right, Karl?"

Karl shrugged. Not all of them were guilty of a crime per se, but all of them were certainly good fuel for the power. And that's all he really cared about. "Of course they are. Now let's go get one. Sheesh, at this hour, anyone out and about is up to no good. You've got a guarantee of that."

An hour later, they'd piled into Robbie's ancient 1973 Chevy work truck. The streets had a slight crust of ice on them. In some spots, there was enough buildup to make the back end slip. But then the snow tires would bite into the pavement and they'd get sorted again. There were few people better at driving in the snow than Robbie, so Karl barely looked up when these momentary missteps occurred. He was thinking hard and trying to channel the power's spirit.

Laz was basically bouncing in his seat. "We ought to get our uniforms on, right?"

Karl grunted sarcastically. "Gee, do you think so?"

Laz missed the sarcasm. "Well seems like people might be angrier to know it was cops that did it, huh?" The sound of him scratching his stubbled face was like a cat on a scarred wood post.

Karl looked at Robbie and rolled his eyes. "What do you think, partner?"

Robbie just shook his head, and the two of them smiled sadly at each other. Karl sometimes thought it was funny how Portland had drawn this incredible and ancient power to its shores and he'd been the one to find it. An eternal and joyous force of absolute strength and capability had come to Portland, and he had found it, and...

He looked behind him at Laz's simple face beaming with energy and sighed. And this was the best he could do. He looked at Robbie, almost to try and convince himself that it wasn't all that bad, but that didn't help so much. Robbie was a decent guy, and he could be mean, and he liked power, but he wasn't from strong stock. Not like Hitler's right hand men.

By the time the three of them had collected their things and gotten dressed (Karl got into uniform simply so Robbie and Laz wouldn't feel alone—he had no plan to be in the tape) it was nearly 3 in the morning. Before he left his house, he went into his bedroom, locked the door at his back just in case one of the boys got curious to poke around after him, and opened up his closet.

His own personal shrine was considerably smaller than the public one they'd erected in Forest Park, but it was no less holy or devout. He could still feel the power here. He had a number of relics to help channel the force: several swastikas, a Nazi flag, some WWII memorabilia, and other historical items from Columbus, King Arthur, the Persians—he even had some lesser known artifacts which he'd paid considerable sums to acquire, which most historians wouldn't have even known about. He kneeled down in the doorway and waited, quietly, for instructions.

Nothing came to him, and after a few minutes, he picked himself up off the floor and went back to join the boys. The power would have let him know if the plan was bad or if he was doing something wrong. It could be assertive when it had to be, but this was surely a good thing. Privately, a little selfishly, Karl thought it would be great fun, too. Stirring up trouble could be immensely pleasurable if you had the right frame of mind to appreciate just how easy it was to get people riled up. The funny thing about these riots was that the felons always burned down their own damn neighborhoods when they got upset. He figured that was like killing two birds with one stone.

They got back into the truck and headed toward Hazelwood. Portland was never quieter than at 3 AM., and even in the bad parts of town where migrants were wandering, all drugged up and drunk, and gang members were still posted up on the corners or skulking around with their pants hanging off their ass, things were pretty still. They rolled down the street like wolves looking for rabbits. Robbie drove slowly, coasting a lot to keep the sound of his engine down. Laz was looking out the back window like a kid on a field trip.

There were policemen actually on duty presently, of course, but none of them would be in Hazelwood at 3 AM., at least not for another half hour or so, and by then, Karl planned to be far away from the scene. His phone was in his pocket, ready to record. From there, it would be easy—drop it onto social media, make sure it was public and shareable. By morning it would be on the news all around America. By tomorrow night he figured they might make global ripples. That's how hot things were right now. Kill a criminal and they'll burn down a damn city. Tragic.

But he didn't care about the public cost. He cared that the power would be fed. The power would be glutted. If he played his cards right —if Robbie and Laz helped him, and some of the other boys at the station who he'd been feeling out, carefully and quietly, were willing to come on board—they'd be able to really create some trouble. Us versus them, it'd nearly come to it already in parts of the city after Floyd and all the others.

Things were never more than a few bad weeks away from absolute pandemonium. Some philosopher or another once said that everyone was three missed meals away from turning savage. He thought that was a bit pessimistic—most people could probably miss more than 3 meals before they bit into their neighbors—but he didn't think it was so far off as to not be interesting to think about.

"There!" Laz hissed, tapping furiously on the foggy window.

Robbie hit the brakes and Karl leaned around his considerable figure to look out of the driver's side window. Sure enough—they'd rolled onto some sort of sordid transaction taking place on the corner of 117th. They weren't too far from the bottle recycling center. The homeless and out of work hung around this place like rats at a factory. Always lots of guys walking around with a couple bucks in their pocket. Why not beg for half? Or hit them over the head if you're really desperate.

Laz was the first out of the truck. He flew like a rabid dog, not even bothering to swing the door. Robbie followed fast. Karl was slower. He wrestled in his pocket for his phone, then got out and managed to turn on the video just as he came to the front of the Chevy.

He caught Robbie and Laz in center frame as they came upon the pair of scoundrels. One of them—the one who'd been rooting in his pocket and pulling out a little baggie—was considerably taller than the average man. He looked a bit like a lamppost without the light. He had on sweatpants and a baggy puff coat; his eyes were dark little circles set into his shadowy face.

Robbie tackled him with a hard grunt, nearly from full speed, and his thin body crumpled up like an inflatable snowman. The other guy was shorter and heavier. He heard Laz coming and braced for him.

Rather than being tackled, he wrapped his arms around Laz's smaller body and started wrestling with him. The two of them began to fight while Robbie laid his whole body on top of Lamppost's crumpled form. He wasn't struggling or trying to get away though. Probably stunned from the impact.

Karl took a few steps closer, to be sure the four of them were in perfect frame. Robbie slapped a pair of cuffs around Lamppost's loose arms and then leapt up to help Laz. A bit of blood was visible, coming from Lamppost's left ear. Karl zoomed in on it for a moment, and then blew the camera back up so the whole scene was visible.

The short man was grunting and jabbering in shock while he tried to shake Laz off of him. "What the hell is wrong with you, man?"

"Get down!" Laz huffed furiously. "Get the hell down!"

But the stocky guy wasn't going to budge. "What are you doing man? You're crazy! I ain't doing anything wrong, I was bumming a smoke. That a crime now?"

Robbie laid a big hand on the guy's arm and started pulling him. He was considerably bigger than Laz, and after taking in the sight of his new opponent from the corner of his eye, the fight seemed to leave the 2nd criminal. He stopped wrestling just as Robbie got a real good grip on him and started to yank him around.

Laz let go and they came untangled. Then he hauled back and cracked the guy across the cheek. The sound of his fist striking bare flesh was satisfying. Karl's heart was beating fast now, and he was trying to keep his breathing quiet.

"Jesus!" he howled, cradling his face and stumbling.

"Jesus isn't here you dimwit," Laz growled heavily. He was breathing hard from the short wrestling match, and he was obviously pissed.

Robbie was a bit calmer. "You got two seconds to kneel before I break your knees and cuff you while you scream for an ambulance."

The guy dropped as if Robbie *had* broken his knees. Just the threat was enough to get him in line.

"Hands behind your back. You're under arrest for—"

"Jack don't look so good man. What the hell did you have to hit him so hard for? Look at him, man! Look at him!"

Karl turned the camera back on Lamppost and clenched his jaw. His body was still in the same spot. The pool of blood growing around his head was considerably bigger. It didn't look like he was breathing. At the very least he was still unconscious.

"Don't worry about him, worry about yourself." Laz came up behind the kneeling felon with his nightstick and cracked him hard across the back of the skull.

It was almost a lazy looking blow, like something done errantly, without much thought. The way a football player would slap his buddies behind when he made a good play. No big deal. Just a lazy crack, enough to make you jump.

But his arm was fully extended, the nightstick was considerably heavier than a hand, and the back of the skull is a notoriously fragile place to hit someone. Something cracked loud—the sound of the bone cracking, like it or not—and a tremendous swell of wind came ripping down from the clouds.

Laz looked up as the stocky fellow fell face first onto the ground and began laughing. He could feel it, too. The power was all around them, swirling, congratulating them on a job well done. It was feeding on the criminals they'd apprehended, drinking up the blood and chewing on the meat. Karl felt an intense, almost orgasmic pleasure as the cold wind circled around them. Robbie looked up and smiled, too.

He held the camera on the two of them as they stood over what was probably the dead bodies of two drug dealers. He was shaking from the pleasure of the power roiling around them. They were like three ships crossing the ocean, and the wind was like waves, carrying them forward and then pulling them back.

He stopped the video as Laz continued laughing.

Big Jim by Igor Beltrame

Forest Park

It was snowing. Big Jim Winthrope stared in disbelief as the white dust came down around them and began to settle on the Douglas-firs and western hemlocks and red cedars that seemed to stretch taller than any skyscraper in the city proper just twenty miles south.

It was 4 PM on November 17th. Too early for snow in Portland. Too early for snow in *Oregon*. But it was snowing. He began to get angry as that fact became more apparent, as a cold wind drove hard through the cottonwoods and western yews and made the violets and morning glory's dance and weave in shock. The bright flowers tried to hug the scrub brush around them. They seemed to think the same thing as him: *what? Snow and cold wind already? It's not fair*!

"How can we be lost?" Mary asked for the fourth time despondently. "Jim, just *how can we be lost in a city park?*"

Big Jim brought his hand up to his mouth and clasped it over his jaw to keep from screaming. He loved Mary, but sometimes, he wanted to kick her like a damn mule. But Big Jim didn't believe in hitting women. Especially not ones he was married to. So he kept his hand there at his mouth and gripped his jaw until his cheeks hurt and he thought he might crack a tooth from grimacing so hard.

"We aren't lost," he said again, checking his watch for the fifth time. Damned if it wasn't *November*. If it were April or May, the sun wouldn't be setting for another couple hours. But it was *November*, and that meant the long shadows looming around them were about to disappear, and rather than cursing at the impending dark, he'd be swallowed by it, like Jonah and the whale.

"Well then why don't you just tell me where we are, Big Jim?"

He scowled at her. She called him Big Jim only when she was terribly angry, or incredibly happy. And just now it didn't take a mind reader to know that Mary was angry as a possum that got its lunch stolen.

He could see the accusations in her eyes. The hurt and the betrayal was worse to him than flung insults or violent curses. *You're supposed to be an outdoorsman*, that frightened and frustrated gaze said. *You used to be a Game Warden, you should know how to navigate a tiny little urban park, you should know how not to get lost, you should know that it gets dark at 4 pm, you should have known to get us back hours ago.*

He zipped up his wind breaker and put his hands on his hips, sighing heavily. It was just a while past 2 PM when he realized he'd chanced upon a trail he didn't know, and that he hadn't seen signage in over an hour. Now, a couple hours later and no closer to understanding where the hell he'd turned wrong or where in the hell he was, he was starting to get a little scared.

Scared not because he thought they were in any real kind of danger. Not even because of the damned snow that was falling at dusk, too early on November 17th at 4:13 PM.

He was getting scared because something had been following them through the midst of Forest Park. And although Big Jim didn't get the name *Big Jim* for nothing—at 240 pounds and 6 foot 4, he was indeed *Big* Jim, he was scared nonetheless, because he had no pepper spray or weapons to speak of, because Forest Park was the site of more than a few grisly murders.

And because whatever was following them was damned big. And it only moved when they did. Like it was smart.

And he had no damned idea where he was. If he screamed, would anyone hear?

"Jim? Are you just going to ignore me?"

He looked at her sternly. "No, Darling. I'm not going to ignore you. I'm just thinking. Can't a man think?"

"You've had over an hour to think, Big Jim Winthrope. Now you finish up thinking and you get us out of here and take me down to the diner and get me a milkshake. I'm tired and my feet hurt and I want to go *home*. We've been out here since nine in the morning! I'm finished! Done! I've had my fill of Forest Park! I've had my fill of Portland, Oregon! I believe I've seen enough of this city to last me a lifetime. There's something wrong with it. I don't want to be here anymore."

He let the tantrum run its course. When she was finished, he nodded sagely, politely. "All right. We'll leave in the morning."

"You're damned right we'll leave in the morning."

He didn't rise to the invitation to engage in an argument. The worst thing to do when you're lost in the wild is argue or panic. There would be time, later, for him to tell her they weren't leaving Portland, Oregon just yet. Because he wasn't done collecting his data, and because the data was absolutely necessary for him to move forward with his paper.

Big Jim was writing a thesis on the biology of northwest vegetation, and had come across troubling mutations in the wilds surrounding the city of Portland that he hadn't been able to explain without putting his boots on the ground. They'd been in the city for a little over a month, and with each sample he got back from the local university labs, the further his research veered off course and began to make no sense.

His earliest theories—that pollution, chemical runoff, or some other kind of man-made screw up had caused the plants to alter themselves in small yet important ways had become harder to prove as the genetic makeup of the plants started to make less and less sense. If he couldn't get it under wraps—something he wouldn't entertain except in his quietest and deepest moments—he'd have to scrap the entire paper and begin a new project.

It wouldn't do. He'd have to figure it all out before they left. Mary would have to deal with it. He'd buy her a nice new watch, or perhaps a pair of earrings, and she'd agree to stay for another week. That's all it would take. Another week and he'd be able to draw up a reasonable causation between the mutations and tuck that chapter away. He'd write a stunning conclusion to the research, carefully describing how it all tied together into what was a *dramatic northwest evolution*, and publish it in *Science Weekly* or perhaps even *The New York Times*, if they'd have him.

"I mean, I don't know where we are, exactly," Jim said harshly, interrupting her for the first time that afternoon, finally losing a bit of his patience. "I do know that Portland is south of us, and that means all we have to do is walk south. And this trail, although I don't know it, *is going south.*"

"You said you knew which trail we were on!" She accused uselessly, as if reminding him that he'd said it would make him suddenly remember the name of the trail and the trajectory of it.

"I thought I did." He grabbed her arm and began to pull her down the curious, unmarked path. It would be good and dark in about 15 minutes. And if the snow didn't stop, they'd be wet and cold.

She ripped her arm free from his grasp. "Don't touch me!"

He obliged, swallowing up his instinct to respond, *you don't have to ask me twice, you fat cow.* One of the reasons he'd brought her out here in the first place was to try and help her get some exercise. Mary had put on over 40 pounds in the last year, and although he still loved her dearly, he couldn't deny that she'd lost all the girlish figure he fell in love with. Still, after they found the right path and got out of here, he'd take her to get a milkshake, just like she asked. Because Big Jim did what Mary asked of him, if he was able. It was why they'd been together for so long.

Beneath the soft patter of the light snowfall, beneath their two stumbling, tired steps, something resumed following them in the brush, just behind and off to the right. Mary couldn't hear it, likely as not, because she was breathing louder than a weed eater that was about to run out of gas. And she'd never spent much time out in the wild like he had, especially not in the north, where being able to hear something bumbling through the brush around you could be the difference between being mauled to death or not.

He looked furtively over his shoulder for the third time. He thought he saw a peculiar, grey shape weaving between a great set of ferns and a pine tree. But no... he squinted, and it was gone. Just the wind. Still, somewhere over there, something was moving. Something far bigger than a squirrel or a raccoon. Something heavy.

Worst thing about it was, he couldn't just stop and investigate. It was near dark, they were lost. It was snowing. An animal might lose interest. If it's territorial, the best thing he could do is put distance between them. Likewise, if it was some kind of murderous lunatic, the best thing he could do is get closer to civilization.

Ignoring trouble—like your wife gaining 40 pounds in just under a year, or being followed by an unknown threat—was something Big Jim found not altogether difficult to do. Often times, he found if you ignored a problem, it simply faded away. It didn't work for cavities, which turned into root canals quicker than you could eat apple pie a la Mode, but it did work for a lot of other things.

He focused on the path. There were only so many steps in a path. One, two, three, four—keep counting, before you get to a billion, you'll be home. That's what he'd been telling himself for the last few hours.

"I'm freezing," Mary whined a couple minutes later. "My shoes are getting wet, Jim."

"So are mine." He brought his hands up to his mouth and blew into them. "Never known it to snow in mid-November in Portland. Bad luck."

She glowered. "I wish you would have brought a map. Or at least let me bring my phone. I could pull us up on GPS and see just where we are, if you had."

He knew that one was coming. He wished he had his phone, too. But if he'd brought his phone, he would have gotten a call. And if Mary had brought her phone, she would have sat down and started playing that damned game with the jewels before it was even time for lunch. Their day would have been ruined by it.

"Nothing to say to that?"

He shook his head. "Nothing good."

She looked up, and a bit of snow fell on her nose and melted. She stuck out her tongue, letting some land there. "I'm thirsty."

"Yeah."

It was good and dark then. It got darker still, somehow, as they kept on forward, being paced evenly by whatever it was that was following them. Jim looked over his shoulder again, almost sneakily. But it was so dark he could barely see more than ten paces away. It was a secretive thing, and shy. It didn't want to be seen.

But it also didn't want to let them go.

A while passed in quiet. Jim could hear it following, never ceasing in its careful pace. The path got wide at one point, and then narrowed so much that he had to push Mary ahead of him and walk behind her. He was mad, but he wouldn't let her walk behind him. Not while there was something unknown behind.

Mary broke the half hour's silence that'd fallen over them, saying, "Jim?"

"We're getting closer now," he said, pretending like he could tell when really, he could not tell at all. This bit of the woods looked just like anywhere else.

"We should have already come upon something," she said evenly. "Think about it. We've been walking for hours now. How long? Three hours? Or four?"

He thought about it, looking down at his watch, which now read 5:30. Yeah. They'd been walking for at least three hours. "That's right."

"Walking pace is just a couple miles an hour, but Forest Park is only eight miles long."

He let the comment hang. It didn't take a mathematician to reason that statement out. Especially considering they hadn't nearly walked clear to the north end of it before coming upon this path, here.

"But paths snake back and forth, Honey." He knew that was true, but still. This trail wasn't snaking. It was mostly straight.

"You always trivialize me," she complained petulantly.

"I don't mean to. But look." He pointed above them, where the branches of a big leaf maple were sprawling and stretching through a red cedar. You could see the sky above, and the moon rising on their right, and—

"God!" he exclaimed suddenly, unable to help himself. "God!" The last thing to do was panic, the last thing he wanted to do was panic. But...

"God!"

Mary grabbed his arm, alarmed. "What is it?"

"The moon's on the wrong damn side of the sky!"

She looked up. "What do you mean?" She hit him on the arm, frightened. "Jim? What do you mean?" She hit him again. "Jim? Answer me!"

He let her go on hitting him, barely even feeling it. The ground was covered in a fine layer of snow, and it wasn't letting up. If anything, the moonlight seemed to illuminate more than a light fall. It was really starting to spit now, like this professor he had in a 1st year seminar, decades and decades ago when he'd been an undergraduate. The front row of that class was conspicuously empty of all but the bravest students.

"We're going the wrong way," he said, stunned, finally voicing the horrible statement just as Mary began to cry. "We're..." he couldn't say it again. The words just couldn't come all the way out. It seemed impossible. Absolutely impossible.

"We're..."

"Jim?" She grabbed him and shook him as hard as she could, which wasn't very hard, but it was enough to make him snap to. "Jim? Are you telling me—"

"We aren't going to get back to Portland tonight," he muttered, barely speaking above a whisper. Two facts fell on him at the same time. He couldn't decide which was more pressing.

That thing which was following him, that thing which he had been expecting to quit rustling through the brush (which, at this precise moment, *had* quit rustling through the brush, because it seemed to do nothing but mirror their movements, and now that they had stopped, it could only stop to match them) had been following them further away from civilization, not closer toward it. And now his working theory— that they had wandered into the territory of a bear, or possibly a mountain lion (although he thought he wouldn't be able to hear a mountain lion) was troubling. Because if that were true, they'd only walked further into its home. It would only, now, be more territorial.

The second fact was a more practical one. And he knew it was true because his wind breaker was wet, and so were his shoes, and his pants were starting to get damp. Even his socks weren't fully dry anymore. The second fact was that you could get hypothermia in temperatures well above freezing if you were wet and it was windy. And right now it was lower than freezing, and he was wet, and would soon be wetter.

And the wind was coming hard—not out of the south, like he thought, but out of the north.

They'd been walking for hours further into Forest Park. Probably, they'd left the actual confines of the park altogether by now, and had walked out of the city limits entirely.

Mary was beside herself. He tuned her out for a while, letting her cry and babble and insult him, and finally, as she started to quiet, he opened his ears to reality again and took a good, hard look at her red, teary face.

"You don't want to go on and cry," he said pitilessly. "We don't have much water left at all."

"You still have water?" she cried indignantly. "I told you hours ago —"

"You drank all yours like a sponge, and I know now you're going to drink all mine the moment I hand it over," he interrupted harshly. "So just you be quiet. All right?"

She gaped at him, and then snapped her mouth closed. It was a rare day when Big Jim spoke harsh to his wife, and although it didn't happen often, she knew that when he did, it was best to be quiet.

He took the hard bottle out of his pack, which was nearly entirely empty of anything at all of use, and shook it a little. It barely had more than a third left. He knew Mary would drink whatever was left in it when it became her turn. So he gulped down what he figured was half, savoring every drop, before handing it to her.

"There," he said as she gulped it down greedily, like a thirsty baby. "There. Just you drink it all."

She gasped, wiping her face with the back of her hand when she was done, and smiled triumphantly. "I will."

He raised his brows. "Feel better?"

She scowled. "No. You've gone and got us lost, Jim! And I'm cold, my feet are wet and they're *tired*!"

He nearly yelled at her, then, but thought better of it. If whatever was out there in the trees—he glanced around nervously, wishing he could see it, expecting to catch the glint of a feral pair of eyes and feeling half relieved when he didn't—heard them fighting, it might take that as a sign of weakness.

"We need to turn around," he said heavily. "This is going to be a long night, Mary. I don't expect you—"

She spun on the spot and began charging back the way they came before he could finish the sentence. There was a thin crust of snow on the path now, and their footprints were clearly marked. She stomped hard in the same spots she'd stomped just seconds ago, and somehow, it was like walking someone back in time.

He followed, jogging a bit to catch up.

He was not surprised when the thing in the brush turned and began to follow them. He focused hard on the sound, trying to make out specific footfalls. But it moved weirdly, almost lumberly. It sounded like it had two legs. But it wasn't tall enough to be a man. He looked back again, just to confirm that. Yes. The brush was moving low to the ground.

A few minutes later, Mary started in again. "Just how do you get turned 180 degree in the wrong direction? Just how does a Game Warden forget which way is north! It's like the punchline to a bad joke, Jim!"

He had a punchline for her, but he didn't think she'd find it very funny. He clenched his fist and breathed heavily through his mouth, as if he could expel the anger along with his bad breath.

"I made a big mistake," he said finally. "And I hope you know that we all make mistakes sometimes. Don't we, Mary?"

She didn't say anything. He thought if he could see her face that it would be puckered up like she'd just sucked on a lemon. Jim normally didn't bring up the affair. It hurt him to talk about it, because it had been the biggest betrayal of his life. It hurt *her* for him to talk about it, because she hated the fact that she'd been caught and that now the fact that she was a liar, and a cheater, was a fact of life and had to be accepted and addressed. She hated that she couldn't talk trash about women on television or in magazines who cheated on their husbands, and act like she was so much better, so much more *moral*.

He realized he had her on the ropes, and went in for the kill. "But I didn't do this on purpose, Mary. Did you think about that? It's not like I did something on purpose, knowing it would hurt you. All right? So do you think you can cut me some slack, Honey? Do you think you could do that for me? Do you think you could be a little *human* and cut me some slack?"

She stopped walking suddenly.

Jim almost bowled her over. Not because he was startled, but because he was getting mad, thinking about all that rotten history, and sometimes when he was mad—

He didn't, though. He stepped to the side quickly, deftly, like he'd known she was going to stop. Because somewhere, he did know. When you're with a woman long enough, you know when you've pushed her over the edge. You know when her brain is going to stop working and she's just going to freeze and clam up and do nothing. Catch her red handed having a year long affair with a man in another country who she's never even met. That'll do it!

Or drag her five hours in the wrong direction in the countries largest urban park while some unknown but large animal is tracking you during the worlds earliest goddamn snow on a windy night. Then bring up some awful thing that neither of you really want to talk about just because your nerves are frazzled and you aren't thinking straight.

He kept walking, trying to make her—perhaps even trying to make himself—believe that he would leave her behind if she didn't kick it back into gear. But he knew he couldn't do that. And so did she.

Maybe thirty paces separated them when he stopped and turned. "All right," he began, "you—"

And that's when the brush exploded.

The thing that burst out at them was grey. Or at least it looked grey in the dark. He only saw a glimpse of it. Erupting out of the woods like a jack-in-the-box, crossing a distance of some fifty feet in a blink. It wasn't a bear or a cougar, it wasn't any thing at all which belonged in Forest Park, or even on planet Earth.

Mary turned as it came. She nearly faced it. And then it was on her.

Jim tried to scream. It wrapped a pair of spindly, slick arms around her, bent its many, skittering legs—and launched itself skyward. A puff of snow went up in the spot where, just a moment before, it had stood with Mary trapped in its grasp.

He blinked and it was gone.

A faint rustle in the treetop made him cringe. He braced for it, began to say a prayer. But nothing came.

It was quiet and still in Forest Park.

A full half minute after the thing had gone, Jim finally became aware of his heart beating in his chest. It was pumping hot, frenzied blood erratically into his trembling arms and legs. Something began to whistle violently, and he only realized it was his own breath wheezing jerkily out of his throat when he started getting lightheaded.

He screamed. Nothing intelligible. Just a raw, terrorized scream that seemed wholly appropriate and reasonable considering the circumstance.

Then he began to shout for Mary. He ran to the spot she'd been in, not caring if it was dangerous. He looked up, into the trees, where the creature had taken her. He tried to convince himself that what he'd seen had not really happened, and then slapped himself in the face for doing something so insane.

He was not crazy. He did not hallucinate. He'd seen it with his own two eyes, less than two minutes ago. One minute per eye. Was that all it took to convince yourself you hadn't seen something frightening? One minute per eye which bore witness?

"Mary!" He screamed, rejecting the notion. He knew what he'd seen. Something had taken his wife. An awful, grey thing, with too many legs, and a face like a man but a body like...

A body like...

"Mary!"

His voice echoed in the empty park. And five hours from civilization, Big Jim Winthrope began to run. He was careful this time to look up, through the snow white branches, and check that the moon was on his left.

He marked it there carefully, consciously, winking at him through the heavy canopy, twinkling as the snow fell beneath it. And then he saw something else. Something that made him wonder, firmly this time, almost guiltily, if perhaps he *had* gone insane.

A gleaming, silver disc came low over the trees. Branches and leaves rustled as it neared. A great wind swept beneath it. A hurricane of snow flew to celebrate its passage. He listened, disbelieving, for the sound of an engine. But it was quiet beneath the disc.

It sailed directly over his head. A huge breeze drove a torrent of snow into his face. A whirlwind of leaf and branch and white powder descended all around him.

He stopped running as it rushed past, twisting around to watch it fly, mouth agape.

A single thought occurred to him, tasting like copper in his mouth. *No one is ever going to publish my paper if I come forward with this.*

As he thought this, so far away he nearly couldn't hear her, Mary screamed.

Big Jim began to run again.

Floater *by Igor Beltrame*

BLACK
WATER
BLUES

Another floater! Katie cursed as the bobbing corpse rolled in the Willamette's current just a few boat lengths off their bow.

Carl knocked the boat's motor into neutral and steered into the wind so they could pull up alongside the unfortunate soul. That brought the breeze over the bloated body and threw the putrefied reek into their faces. Carl cried out and brought his arm up to cover his face.

Once upon a time, that smell would have gotten to her, too. But she'd been patrolling the Willamette with the Multnomah County River Patrol long enough that all it did was make her curl her lip. It wasn't technically any less offensive than the first time she smelled it— she was just prepared for the stench now. Not unlike gaining an acquired taste for a food you hate.

Once, she'd have felt sorry for the corpse, too. She leaned over the bow and dropped the cage into the water at just the right angle to gobble the body up. Carl came up to help her, still shielding his face. He was squinting, too, as if he could make the body any less gross looking by screwing up his eyes. Together they hauled it aboard in the aluminum cage specially designed for this grisly task.

"Do you reckon his family—"

"Let's not go over this again," Katie interrupted sharply. Carl was an incessant chatterer. Most of the time she didn't mind, but the minutes after pulling a body aboard were moments she liked to spend in silence. There was a lot a body could tell you if you learned to look at it. The water was cold enough, especially this time of year, to preserve a lot more than you'd think. Even after it had ballooned.

She forced herself to look at the gassy, bloated mound of flesh that used to be a human being. White pus flesh, a good amount of which had been nibbled away by fish—a broken vase of a nose that now revealed the inside of a mostly hollow skull. A lipless mouth that gaped to reveal a few dozen rotting teeth, hands that were missing fingers and swollen and split; a pair of tattered jeans that were more gone than present.

Surprisingly, "he's still got his shoes."

Carl snorted. "Pretty rare."

Katie might have corrected him and said it was around 50-50, but she didn't want to argue. She was really just thinking out loud anyway. But the shoes always made her suspicious. Jumpers would take their shoes off at whichever bridge they were leaping from more often than not. It wasn't a guarantee of anything, but it indicated foul play. Lately, the mix of bodies that put themselves in the river was starting to get overshadowed by those that seemed to have gone in with a struggle.

Something was happening in Portland. As she looked at the dead man through the wire bars of the retrieval cage, that fact sunk in more firmly than it had in all the weeks leading up to that moment, for no particular reason. She'd been working it over in her head for a long time—maybe all year—and maybe this was the final straw. Something told her certainly, positively, that this man was one of the men that had ended up in the river for mysterious reasons.

"He was married," Carl observed, unaware he was interrupting her deepest reckoning.

He was right, though. The victim's finger had swelled until it burst around his wedding ring. Likewise, the Rolex on his wrist broke and split the bloating flesh of his hand and arm. "He was well off, too. If he's not a missing person, that pretty well concludes foul play. Let's call him in."

"Want to check for a wallet?"

She scowled. Carl was always happy to break rules. He'd been especially resistant to those pesky things folks like her called *laws* ever since he joined her on River Patrol. All just to sate his own curiosity. It's not like they wouldn't find out soon enough. "No more touching than necessary. Forensics will take over soon. *Call him in.*"

Carl grumbled defensively, but did as he was told.

Katie walked to the bow and perched at the extreme edge of the boat. The river was wavy this morning, and she felt a bit like an old sailor riding the swells in the Atlantic. Of course the Willamette was nothing compared to the open ocean. But the wind was picking up and clouds were gathering in the sky. She looked for the sun and thought she could see it hiding behind a particularly heavy grey haze.

Half an hour later, they pulled into the dock and forensics was waiting for them. How many times this month had they been through this procedure? How about this year? She shook her head, not wanting to count, but also realizing it might finally be time *to* count. Something about this one—the watch or the ring, maybe, or perhaps he was just the proverbial dead body that made the dead body cart topple over— had made it all snap together for her.

Something was seriously wrong in Portland. There were more dead bodies floating in their river every month than the rest of the country's rivers combined. The rest of River Patrol talked about the uptick like it was nothing more than an especially rainy season. But the longer Katie mulled over it, the more their reactions were bugging her. Dead bodies weren't weather. Something had to be happening to put them there.

She felt a peculiar and undeniable attachment to the disgusting corpse as forensics lifted it, cage and all, off the boat. Carl was up on the dock, chatting with another River Patrol crew. It sounded like they were cracking their usual jokes. Katie didn't have the energy to hiss at them. They were all just trying to normalize it, and who could blame them? It was nasty business, what they had to do.

She disembarked and swaggered down the wooden slats. Carl nodded at her as she neared. Davey, her old mentor, and a new trainee called Gregor were spectating the forensic crew bustling about with their new body.

"How's it going Captain Katie?" Gregor joked. He was well over six feet tall, and weighed about 100 pounds more than he should have if he were healthy. But he was jovial and red faced and always impossibly positive. She didn't mind the ribbing.

"It's going," she replied. Then she turned serious before anyone could drag her into small talk. "Listen, something about this one doesn't sit right with me. When you ID him, call me on my personal as soon as you can. All right?"

Davey, who was nearly the opposite of Gregor in every way—short, thin, bespectacled, and well mannered—blinked at her curiously. "What's got you thinking, Katie?"

She glanced at Carl and Gregor, feeling defensive, before answering Davey honestly. "This whole year has me thinking. We've fished more bodies out of the river since New Year's than we did in the last two years combined. And a hell of a lot of them have gone unsolved, haven't they? More than usual, I mean."

Carl grimaced. "You're not trying to knock our numbers down even further than they already are, Katie, are you? Come on, the precinct—"

She could give a rat's ass about the precinct. "The precinct wants to solve crimes, not look good for the city. *And there are crimes happening right under our noses!*"

Gregor rubbed his face comically and scrunched up his nose. "Yikes!"

Davey elbowed him. "Don't prod her, boys. Katie's right. But..." he hesitated, sighing, looking over his shoulder as if to double check that they were alone at the far end of the dock. When he confirmed that they were—the pair of students from Portland University volunteering that day were lugging the bloated body back to the van—he continued, "...but I'm going to warn you that if you stick your nose in this one, you might not like how it smells. Literally and figuratively."

She stared. "What do you mean?"

"I mean—" he looked over his shoulder again "—I mean that something bad is obviously going on. This uptick is beyond the statistical norm. There's no good explanation for this."

Carl and Gregor exchanged glances, but Katie ignored them. The two of them combined weren't half as clever as Davey. She looked at the diminutive man who taught her most of what she knew about River Patrol with a raw intensity she normally reserved for the bedroom. "What do you know?"

"Nothing yet," he protested sternly, looking away in a telltale way which indicated to Katie that he was concealing something. "Nothing at all. But I'm suspicious, same as you. And common sense tells me that whatever's happening is dangerous. If you make noise and look around where you're not supposed to be, it might be *you* we're fishing out of this river."

Carl couldn't keep quiet any longer. "You two are trying to make something out of nothing."

Gregor hummed his agreement. "You know how much work you're going to make for us if you start trying to investigate every gas-sack floating in the Willamette as a murder, Kate?"

She bared her teeth at him like a bad dog. Everyone used humor to cope, but something about the phrase *gas-sack* was too much, even for her. "Could you be a bigger pig?"

"I'm just telling it like it is," he says, unperturbed. "More work for us would be the best case, and what Davey's saying is the worst. What if I'm wrong, huh? Then you'd end up getting embroiled in something big. Something best left to the FBI or maybe even the CIA, Jesus, what do we know? Forensics ought to figure out the truth of it, and—"

"*Forensics is too worried about buggering up our stats!*" she hissed, both aware that her voice was getting too loud and unable to stop it at the same time.

Davey looked anxiously toward the van. The college kids were just now closing the back. The two senior forensic guys were standing over them like overseers. They didn't appear to have heard her shout.

Carl scoffed at her. "You think they're suppressing evidence?"

She lifted her chin defiantly. "Of course they are!"

"I think I'd better take my leave," Gregor said swiftly. "You're going to make me sick. Whose side are you on, anyway?" He shook his head and started to walk back to the van, seeming disgusted.

She suppressed her first urge, which was to run after him and hit him in the back of the head, and then her second urge, which was to scream an insult. Davey looked after him sadly, and then apologized on his behalf:

"He's loyal to the Patrol, Katie. You understand, right?"

"I understand all right," she said, wanting to sound venomous but failing due to the worried look on Davey's face.

"He's still learning," Davey explained weakly, as if he was personally responsible for everything Gregor said or did. "I gotta go. But before I do—"

She waved his warning away before he could give it. "I'll be careful. But I'm not just going to pretend it's not happening." She glared at Carl, who, despite his not being the brightest or the most ethical, could normally be relied on to back her up, and had failed totally to do that in this event. "I'm going to do my job."

Davey nodded soberly and went after Gregor with a parting request. "You've got my number. Give it a ring this weekend. We'll talk."

She watched him go, and then turned on Carl. But he already looked a little guilty and sad, so she didn't lay into him. Instead, she asked him a question. "You're really not curious about what's happening around here? Come on, Carl, you've got to admit... it's suspicious. We've pulled so many dead men out of the river this year it's starting to get hard to remember their faces. I have to actually break into the filing cabinet and pull out the reports to keep them straight now. You know how wrong that is?"

He breathed heavily. "I just don't want to make any waves, Kate. You know I'm looking to get promoted, and—"

That did it for her. He was really looking after himself before he looked after the people of Portland? Before he looked after the city they were supposed to be serving and protecting? She couldn't keep the look of revulsion off her face, and Carl could see it plain.

"Hey, don't look at me like that. I've got a family to take care of, and—"

"Save it," she spat. She was already walking down the dock, nearly at a jog. Let him deal with the boat. If her own partner didn't have faith in her, if the Patrol at large didn't have faith, then she'd figure it out alone.

But first, she needed to blow off some steam. Maybe it'd be best to wait until they got Rolex's autopsy back, anyway. Then she'd see what connections she could string together between him and the other files she'd tucked away in her desk. A good half of them were marked SUICIDE or ACCIDENTAL DROWNING, but she could read between the lines better than the general public.

She drove to the gym, thinking so hard the whole way that when she pulled into the nearly deserted parking lot, she realized she didn't remember passing a single stop sign or stop light on the whole drive. She shook her head as she put the car in park, trying to wake herself up a little. It wasn't good to get lost in thought like that while driving. She'd read a study once that said driving like that was almost like driving drunk.

Fortunately, wrapping up her hands and putting on her old worn out boxing gloves didn't require as much attention as driving. She strode past the few guys who were serious enough about their bodies to be at the gym before lunchtime and claimed the far corner where the heavy bag was waiting to take some punishment. Then she fell into her old rhythm, jab, jab, hook, slip—hitting the heavy bag was as much upper body as it was lower. She jumped left and right, weaved, sunk low and went high, engaging her core. She threw hooks with both arms. She fought southpaw for a few minutes, then slipped back to her orthodox stance.

After a few rounds, she started throwing kicks. Her hands always got sore these days after 10 or 15 minutes, and they were the only pair of hands she was ever going to get, so she'd decided to protect them as best she could. The old heavy bag shook the rafters of the gym when she landed proper kicks, too, and that made it more satisfying than punching. She fought an imaginary 6 round fight, which was as much as she could force herself to do so early in the morning. When she was done, she declared herself the winner and went to the fountain to get a drink.

A tall black guy who'd been lifting free weights when she first got there was already at the fountain. He nodded at her as she walked up and moved out of the way. His face was freshly shaved and sweaty. He had a face that made it hard to tell if he was 20 or 40. His body looked more like it was 20—but when she looked into his eyes, she thought they were the eyes of a seasoned adult. Something about him looked familiar, but she couldn't put her finger on it. Did he look like a celebrity?

She could tell he was going to talk to her before she leaned down to take a drink.

"Did you win your fight?"

She took her time drinking before straightening up, wiping her mouth with the back of her arm, and smiling at him. "I fought to a hard draw, but I was the underdog, so that's a victory in my book." She hesitated, trying to sort it out for herself, then voiced her curiosity aloud. "Hey, we don't know each other, do we? You look familiar."

He shook his head *yes*. "You came to my sisters funeral." He stopped, like he wasn't going to keep going, then scratched his jaw and added, "damn, I guess that was nearly 6 months ago. Doesn't seem like it's been 6 *weeks*."

His answer disarmed her for longer than she'd thought it would. For 5 or 6 immeasurably long seconds, she simply stared at him. Then it hit her—just about as hard as she'd been hitting the heavy bag—*his sister was one of the floaters in the Willamette*. Forensics had declared her an ACCIDENTAL DROWNING, but that hadn't been right, had it? No.

He was perceptive enough to see the pain on her face. "Didn't mean to dredge up a bad memory. I figured, what, with your line of work, you're probably pretty numb to it."

"I am—" she stopped herself and shook her head "—well, I was at one point. It's harder now." She faltered, looking around them to see who else in the gym might be listening. But there were only two other people inside at this hour, and both of them were across the building, lifting weights.

"Do you know something about her case?" he asked, suddenly intense. "I never thought it made sense, you know? She knew how to swim, even if she had fallen in. It's—"

"The currents are powerful," Katie said reflexively. She hated herself the moment the lame line came out, because that's the type of shit they said at the precinct to keep everyone in line and make sure no one asked too many questions. She didn't even believe it herself. It was true that the currents were powerful, but it was also true that, up until a year ago when the amount of bodies found in the Willamette more than doubled, drowning was rare.

He raised his brows at her, and then hung his head and sighed. "Truth is, I haven't thought about her in a few weeks. It was hard at first, you know? But... I don't know, I guess a few months ago, I realized I'd gone a day without having her on my mind. I don't want to forget, I'll never forget. But I want to be able to turn it off for a while if I need to. Know what I mean?"

Katie nodded fervently, feeling weirdly connected to the guy, whose name she'd forgotten. "Of course. That's all any of us want when something bad happens. To be able to forget it. Even just for a little while."

"When I saw you though?" He breathed heavily and grunted. "Whew! It all came back. And you know what I thought?"

She bit her tongue, feeling like he was about to say something that would root her deeper and more firmly than she already was. "What'd you think?"

"I thought, *none of that shit ever did seem right*. Took me a while to really settle on that feeling, you know. The shock of it all was the biggest thing for a few weeks. But then I really got to thinking. None of us believe Miranda fell into the river and drowned. We talked it over, really went over the case. Not a damn one of us. But the fucking police —" he smiled apologetically "—you know, those forensic assholes, not you. They wouldn't hear a thing of it."

Katie leaned down to take another drink to hide her face. This whole chain of events seemed like an impossible and extraordinary circumstance. How unlikely was it, really, that the very place she came to get her mind off the bodies and the cases, was holding an undeniable reminder of one of the most suspicious and peculiar *accidents* that happened this year?

She straightened up suddenly and made a declaration without bothering to think it through. "I'm going to look into Miranda's case again."

Now it was his turn to look surprised. He stared for a few seconds, totally nonplussed. "Huh?"

"I'm saying I agree with you." In the back of her mind she wondered how many laws she was breaking right now, and just how many agreements she'd signed about not talking about cases after they were closed, especially not with the victim's family, were being violated. But she didn't care. She'd come to the gym to get her mind off things, and instead she'd been slapped right in the face with a cold reminder that things couldn't be forgotten about. Not unless she left Portland for good. And she wasn't ready to do that.

"You think something else happened to her?"

"I think..." she caught herself before she went too far and chuckled humorlessly. "I think I'd better hold my tongue. But Miranda's case never sat right with me, if you want the truth. And there have been a few others since then."

He looked like a man who'd been kicked in the groin. "You think there's a connection?"

"Maybe..." one of the guys at the far end of the gym started to rack up his weights and head their direction, and she nodded to the parking lot. "Listen, why don't we exchange numbers? I'd like to be able to reach out if I have any questions. Would that be all right?"

He picked up his gym bag off the floor and shouldered it grimly. "Yeah. But you'd better be serious about this. Don't go getting my hopes up and then fall limp on me. I don't think I could stand that."

"I'm serious all right," she said, and whether from the look on her face or the conviction in her tone, she saw he believed her.

On Sunday, while she was lounging in her underwear at home and watching reruns of a show she'd seen a thousand times, her phone started ringing. The shrill note of her stupid ringtone shot a lance of pain straight down the back of her head. She drank entirely too much whiskey last night, trying to drown the incessant whirling machine of this mystery.

She fumbled with it, dropping it to the floor and only managing to drag her finger across the screen to answer it after three or four rings had gone off.

"Hello?"

It was Carl. "Katie? You sound like shit. Did you just wake up?"

"I've been up for two hours, I'm just shrugging off a hangover. What's your excuse?"

"I'll plead guilty to my crimes before a jury of my peers. No excuse."

That got a smile out of her. Imagining Carl being charged with grand larceny or some other such crime was fun. "Finally ready to own up to all your wrongs? That's big of you."

He chuckled. "I was actually calling about work. You got a minute? We can just talk about it Monday if—"

She sat up straighter and stopped him before he could talk himself out of it. "I've got a minute. What's going on?" It was entirely out of character for Carl to want to talk about work on the weekend. Come to think of it, he'd only ever called her once or twice since they'd met, and both of those times it'd been for totally obscure matters.

"It's about that bloater we pulled up on Friday. You know, Rolex?"

Her heart started beating fast. It's like she couldn't get away from the work even when she tried. Was this some kind of cosmic call from above, willing her to step fully into the mystery and solve it at all costs? Every time she tried to distance herself, something peculiar happened to put her back into the midst of it.

"What about him?"

"Well, I guess Davey might call to tell you himself, but there is a bit of a mystery with that one." His voice took on a begrudging tone and he added, "You were right after all."

The one time he had information she really wanted to know and he was being vague and slow. "Go on, I don't have all day."

"Don't you? Who—"

"Carl!"

"Fine," he relented. "I guess the guy's been missing for about a month, but forensics say he'd only been dead for a few weeks at most. His family reported him MIA after he didn't come home from work. They're officially declaring it a homicide, although cause of death isn't clear yet."

Her interest was officially piqued. That thing called *chance* was starting to fade rapidly and give way to something called *method*, or maybe even *pattern*. This was the exact same story they'd had with Miranda, and two or three other floaters if memory served her correct. "You realize this isn't the first time this has happened, right?"

She heard him groan into the phone. "Oh, don't get all freaky on me. I was just calling to say thanks—you saved my butt when you told me not to check his wallet. I guess your instincts aren't always wrong, huh?"

She knew he was mostly mocking her, but she didn't care. Call this the proverbial straw that snapped that camel's spine like a dry piece of kindling—whatever—she was head over heels, now. Forget the gym, forget the boxing gloves, forget driving with your mind so full of thoughts that you might as well be drunk. She was going to solve this damn mystery. Not for Rolex, not even for Miranda—but for all the bastards at River Patrol who would rather close their eyes tight than do their jobs.

She hung up on Carl without bothering to reply to his open ended statement. Maybe in his mind, calling her like this was a way to say sorry and admit he was wrong. Or maybe it was just his idea of a good joke. But she didn't have time for him anymore. She didn't have time for anyone that was going to detract from her goal.

Something awful was going on in Portland. She decided then, at that moment, sitting on the couch in her underwear with last nights hangover finally starting to fade, that she was going to get to the bottom of it. No matter what. Even if it meant floating in the Willamette herself.

After digesting that realization, she dialed Davey. The old man let it ring long enough that she thought it was going to voicemail. When he picked up, he sounded out of breath, but not distressed.

"Katie?"

She started in at once. "I just talked to Carl. I want to see Rolex's autopsy. Can you get it for me?"

He made a noise that was barely audible through the phone. Then he said, "I've already got it. I can send it over to you, if you'd like. I'm not sure you'll find much on the surface worth value, though. Not unless you've got other cases on hand to compare it with."

"This is all connected," she said heatedly. "Of course there's nothing on the surface. But somewhere underneath…" she faltered. For a few seconds, she was totally unsure how to phrase it. Then she pressed forward as best she could "…somewhere underneath the surface, lost down in the dark water of the Willamette, there's something to tie this all together, Davey. *I know it.*"

He was quiet for a while. "Well, if you're right or wrong, I'm happy to send over the report. Can I tell you something, though, before I do?"

She told him to make it fast.

"You grew up here, right?"

"Lake Oswego," she admitted. "Close enough."

"So you care about Portland. You consider it your home."

"Of course I do," she said guardedly. "I care about people being murdered and dumped in the river, too, unlike just about every damn asshole we work with. Look, if you're going to try and talk me out of this, just save your breath."

"I'm not going to try and talk you out of it," he said impatiently. "I'm going to warn you that there's a lot going on in Portland behind the scenes. Things I'm not even going to pretend to know about."

She thought about the warning for a moment, and thinking brought up a question of her own. "Now it's my turn. Let me ask *you* something."

She could hear the reluctance in his voice. "Go on."

"Friday at the dock when we pulled Rolex in, you seemed like you knew something but didn't want to say it. Are you holding out on me? Have you figured something out?"

"There's a connection all right," he said, surprisingly forthcoming considering he hadn't offered the information before she asked. "I've seen the files at your desk, you know? Most of the ones you've centered in on are part of it, as far as I can tell, but you've missed quite a few."

That got her pulse up. So Davey knew something was up. Davey believed her. He'd even gone so far as to already draw lines between cases and make conclusions. She felt vindicated and betrayed at the same time. If he knew anything—even just a theory—why wouldn't he have shared it without making her drag it out of him?

"One other thing," he said when she didn't reply. "Don't go poking around anywhere you shouldn't. At least not without giving me a call first."

She started to reply only to realize the call had been disconnected. She stared at the phone for a few minutes afterward, trying to sort through everything Davey had said. There was an undeniable feeling creeping up in her belly that he knew more than he was willing to say. He'd been open enough in admitting there was a connection in the cases, but the warnings were something else. What was he afraid she was going to discover? Where was he afraid she was going to go?

She got up to make coffee. While it was boiling, she washed her face, put on a tattered tank top and some old sweats, brushed her teeth, and put her hair up in a hat. Then she poured herself a cup, mixed in a tiny bit of milk, and opened up her laptop.

She had an email from Davey, just as he promised. It was the most recent, and therefore at the top. Something kept her from clicking it immediately. She moused over the ones below it, none of which were interesting enough to follow up on, and then circled back to Rolex's autopsy. Davey had titled the email: *we all float in the Willamette,* which must have been his idea of a joke.

She opened the email and clicked to download the attachment. Her wireless spazzed for a few seconds before agreeing to do the work she demanded of it. Then the PDF was there in the bottom corner of the browser, waiting to be viewed.

She bit her tongue and opened it. Rolex's name was Michael Shell. He was 46, from California, and a doctor. The postmortem showed he'd been in the Willamette between 10 and 14 days, which means he'd been off the grid for around two weeks before he ended up there. What happened in the interim was anyone's guess, but he had a broken rib and clavicle, which wasn't good. Depending on how he got into the river, that could have happened from falling. That wasn't likely, though.

She scanned through the document a second time, ignoring the pictures as best she could. What had Davey seen here that connected Rolex to the other cases? Other than the fact that he was missing before he died, she was coming up blank. She minimized the PDF and searched through her files, going months back, to find Miranda. She wasn't supposed to have this stuff on her personal PC, but who the hell cared? Certainly not anyone at the precinct, certainly not anyone at River Patrol.

She'd been through this report a hundred times it seemed like. At first glance, nothing stood out. But then she saw it, nestled inconspicuously beside the occupation line: Miranda was a marketer at Pfief Subsidiaries. Where had she read that before?

She opened Rolex's autopsy again and read fast. He was a doctor, yes, but not at a hospital. He worked in the research lab at Pfief. He was a scientist, a researcher. He worked at the same place as Miranda.

She wracked her brain for the last suspicious death, but the thoughts were whirling too quick for her to remember anything specific. She combed through her files instead and landed on one pretty quickly: Joe Harbor. He'd barely been more than a kid, 22 or 23. Friends and family described him as the happiest guy alive. Just like Miranda and Rolex, there was a period of time between his reported death and him having gone missing.

She skimmed until she landed on occupation, and gasped like someone slapped her. He was a fucking janitor at—you guessed it—*Pfief Subsidiaries.*

She called Davey. This time he picked up on the first ring.

"I guess—"

"What in the hell is going on at that place?" she exploded. "And why the hell isn't the FBI and the CIA and every other law enforcement agency knocking on their doors to figure out how half a dozen employees have wound up dead in less than a year? How many more are there, Davey? How many more?"

"You're not asking the right question." He breathed heavily into the phone, almost like a chuckle, but she could tell he didn't find anything funny.

"How many people work for this place? Where the hell even is it? I've never seen a building with that name on it."

"There you go," he said vacantly. "That's the ticket. *Where the hell even is it?* That's what I've been asking myself for a few weeks, ever since I noticed the connection."

She was already typing the name into her search engine. Google tried to correct her spelling—as if Pfief wasn't a real business or organization, as if the name were meaningless and not tied to any organization that actually existed. She narrowed the search: Portland, Pfief Subsidiaries, and still came up blank.

She was starting to get scared. "Davey? What is this shit? It's listed clear as day on their autopsies, so this place can't be that secret."

"It's not a secret. But there's also not a trace of this place existing on the internet, Katie, and I find that damn odd. You know what else? It's not in the phone book, the national registry, it's not on any list of businesses in the city. How do they hire employees? I haven't got a clue, cause I've searched job postings and newspapers and magazines, too."

"This is a smoking gun," she cried. "*How many people who've ended up in the Willamette worked there?*"

"I don't rightly know. So many of the files get stored away. I only got wise a few months ago."

"You've been looking into this for months and you never thought to say anything to me?" She was hurt. Davey had trained her when she first came to River Patrol, nearly a decade ago. She thought he trusted her. They went back further than plenty of folks had been working the job.

"I didn't know what I was getting into," he said calmly. "And I didn't want to pull you into something bad. But then you started asking questions, and well, I think I could use a little help, if I'm honest."

She decided to let it go. "Fine. What do you know about this place?"

"It's backed by old money," he said readily. "And highly secretive. Private company, but I think they've got ties to the federal government, too. Perhaps something they're making—I don't know. I think Rolex is one of the first victims that might have actually been high up in the chain. He definitely knew what was going on in there."

"Can you show me where it is?"

He thought about that for a long time. Katie had to check to make sure the phone hadn't disconnected. Then she heard his voice come reluctantly from the speaker: "If you're willing to go into work on your day off, sure. It's inaccessible from land, but you can get a pretty good view from the water."

An hour later they were disembarking from the dock on an official River Patrol vessel. It was cold out, so they were bundled up in their warmest jackets and gloves. Once they got up to speed, the wind coming off the top of the river was cold enough to turn their noses and ears numb. Her eyes were watering from the dry air.

Davey sat in the pilot's seat, and she stood next to him, shivering a little. Neither of them said much. They were about the same height, which was to say Davey wasn't tall. But he had a gun on his hip—something River Patrol didn't normally carry on the water—and when she saw him get out of his car at the precinct, she thought, *Davey doesn't look like someone I'd want to mess with today.*

"How'd you end up finding this place?"

"Broke every rule and regulation in our handbook," he said bluntly. "Harassed families, tailed people who'd committed no crimes, Jesus, I made about a hundred cold calls. Finally I got a good lead from a sanitation worker. Even secret facilities have to do upkeep."

She raised her brows. Davey had been a detective before River Patrol, so she wasn't surprised. Still, she wasn't sure she would have been able to do that on her own. "I'm impressed."

"You should be."

They ripped through South Portland going north. Katie looked at the city differently as they cut through the water. It had become a darker place in her mind these last few months. That day, it looked to her like a different place entirely.

"I didn't even bother to ask how far it was," she realized.

"An hour, at least." Davey shrugged at the look on her face. "We're on the clock, and doing our job, anyhow. Someone jumped earlier today. Keep your eyes out."

For the rest of the ride, she scanned the waters for a bobbing body. But they were far outside the probable zone the current might have taken the victim—he'd jumped miles and miles back—so she knew all the while that she wouldn't chance upon anything. At least not anything anyone expected.

Sometimes, the currents would pull a body deep into the inky waters and hold it down there for weeks or even months. Other times, a body would float on the surface, or just beneath the surface, for days or weeks and ride deep down the river. Bodies from Portland had floated all the way into the Columbia and out to sea. It wasn't even impossible for them to end up down the coast.

Finally, long after they'd left the bulk of the city behind, Davey knocked the throttle into neutral and pointed starboard. The shore was sloping where he pointed, and rocky all along the river. It would be impossible to pull up and disembark. There was a fence about a hundred yards from the water, anyway, at least 10 feet tall and wired at the top.

"It looks like a prison," she said, awestruck. "How in the world has no one asked any questions about this place?"

"Who would they ask?" Davey pondered, shrugging. "And really, does it look so conspicuous? It *could* be a prison, for all anyone knows. Who would care?"

That didn't sit right with her, though. It was a gaudy place. Beyond the fence, the back of Pfief's compound was clearly visible. It had sweeping glass windows from floor to ceiling and was several stories tall.

Curiously, there was a wide sewage pipe, nearly big enough to drive a boat into, running down from the belly of the compound straight into the river. It was impossible to tell what came out of it, but her mind immediately went to chemical spills and waste. Why else would they have installed something like that, if not to dump things into the water?

"That should have gotten someone's attention at the city," she said. "No way that's legal."

"I'm sure it has," Davey agreed. "And they've probably greased a hundred palms to keep it there."

"Just how much money could they have? What are they doing in there?"

"Experiments," he said plainly. "I thought that was clear."

She grumbled. "But what kind of experiments?"

Davey shook his head. "Ones worth killing over, apparently."

Katie sat down at the front of the River Patrol boat and breathed heavily. What was she supposed to do with all this information? Who could she take it to? What did any of it even mean?

"There's something going on in that building," Davey said after a few minutes had passed. "I've talked to some old friends at the station about it. No one will touch it. I've put in a dozen anonymous tips. Near as I can tell, they throw them straight in the trash. The place is immune."

"Do you think they see us out here? We don't exactly blend in."

"I hope so," Davey growled, glaring up at the glass window with a scowl. "I damn sure hope so. Let them sweat a little."

"They could be dangerous," she mused, not really scared.

"So can we."

She grinned at Davey when he said that, because she could tell he really meant it. He was outraged and hurt and offended, just like she was. Knowing she wasn't alone at River Patrol in wanting justice meant the world to her.

"So you've come out here before?"

"Twice," he admitted. "Once at night. I got spooked though and sped off."

"Scared? You? The great Captain Davey of River Patrol?"

He cut the engine and leaned over the edge of the water. They were a good stone's throw offshore, and the full stretch of river was silent and bare. It was just them and whatever weirdos might be looking at them from inside Pfief's glass walls.

He seemed distracted and curious. "Come over here and look down in the water."

She drew up next to him cautiously. They were perfectly parallel to the pipe running out of Pfief's belly. Davey was leaning far enough over the boat that she could have easily pushed him in.

"What do you see?"

"I don't know," he said, clearly befuddled. "Thought I saw something moving down there. I thought—" he jolted and drew back. "God!"

She drew back too, mostly out of fear of his reaction. She didn't see anything in the dark water. "What is it? I don't see shit."

He was breathing heavy enough that she knew he was really scared. "*Look.*"

She strained her eyes to see deeper into the muddled waters. What could have scared him so much? Davey had seen a thousand dead bodies. What could be worse?

"What is it, Dave?"

He leaned back over a little, still breathing heavily out of his mouth. "It's *moving* Kate! *It's moving. Like a damn zombie*!"

For a second, she still wasn't sure what he meant. Then she saw it: a flash of moving flesh. At first she thought it was a river trout's belly. Then she saw the seaweed stranded hair and the bulging eyes, and screamed.

Prey *by Arika Chamberlain*

No Breath

It was raining out. Later, after it was all over, he'd remember the way the rain pooled and sloshed in the potholed streets as he ran through the city. He'd remember how cold it was with the water splashing all the way clear up to the back of his shirt. He'd remember how loud it was. Portland was a loud city all on its own, but add a thunderous rainstorm to the mix, and then add the sound of your own blood roaring and twanging in your ears. The sound of your lungs inflating and deflating as rapidly as they've done since middle school, and the sound of a dozen police sirens screaming like panthers zipping down just about every street within a square mile, and well, you might begin to understand just how loud it was while Lee was running through the wet streets that night.

He didn't notice, then, that it was wet. He didn't notice it was loud, either. He didn't even notice it was dark, or cold, or windy. He didn't notice he could barely breathe or that his chest was stinging or that his heart felt like it was going to beat right through his ribs and rip out of his chest like an alien. He didn't notice that his eyes were bulging or that his left tennis shoe had finally given out and split down the big toe seam.

He noticed that no matter how much he wanted to run toward the Steel Bridge which led to North Portland that he was being irresistibly and uncontrollably drawn toward Asylum Avenue. Even as the sirens were whirling a street down from him and the police lights were bouncing down the alleyways and a young couple was coming out of a late night diner, even as he could feel the full weight of the world coming down on his shoulders, even as her blood was still warm on his hands—a few more minutes and it'd be washed away in the rain, washed away forever down a million drains and sewers and pumped into the river and then...

The couple heard him coming. They turned at what he could only assume was the sound of a huffing and puffing madman charging headlong down the sidewalk like a lunatic—the woman drew back slightly behind the man—and then he was on them. He didn't bother trying to go around. It would have been quicker if he could have avoided them, but he felt like running them over would be better. He didn't know why. He just did. Lee learned a long time ago to listen to his instincts and give in to the whispers that ate away at the back of his psyche. Things worked out for him when he did.

He dropped his shoulder into the guys chest. He was a tall guy, and a little portly, but he was standing still and Lee was running as fast as he'd ever run in all his life and that meant he bowled him over like a bowling ball knocks down pins. His girl went flying into the street and a car slammed on the brakes and tires skid and the man groaned and shouted as he fell. The girl screamed something, too, but her sound was high pitched like the tires squealing and so it was mostly lost. Sound was a funny thing in that way, not at all like sight or smell.

Lee kept on running, only slightly off balance. He didn't even look back to admire his handiwork. He didn't have any time to look back.

And the sirens kept wailing into the night. Closer now, and then further away, and then closer again. A police cruiser whipped down a side street just a bit in front of him—how hard it would be to avoid them if they had their lights and sirens off, he didn't want to imagine.

Fortunately, they were Portland police, and that meant they were about as capable of catching a man like him as a wiley coyote is capable of catching a roadrunner. He had plenty of time to dive between a stained brick wall and a dumpster before it ever turned and shined its headlights down the road he was running on.

He tried to catch his breath as the cruiser came ripping down the street. It was a lion in hot pursuit of a gazelle, or a shark swimming fast in a shallow reef after a juvenile seal. How in the hell did this happen? That's what he was asking himself as he wheezed and gasped behind the dumpster. How did it end up like this? He'd picked up twenty women before this one, and it'd always gone off without a hitch.

Tommy wouldn't have turned him in. That didn't make sense. He'd been buying girls from Tommy for nearly a decade now. Tommy was nearly his best friend, even though Tommy didn't know his name and he knew Tommy wasn't *actually* Tommy's name—even though they didn't even know each other's names or where each other lived or what each other did in their spare time or even where the other one was from, (he thought from the accent that Tommy was European, but he couldn't say for sure) they were like friends and friends didn't rat you out to the police.

Tommy was a trafficker, and that was another point in his favor. What the hell would a sex trafficker be calling the police on one of his clients for? Lee always paid upfront, in good cash, and he'd never once tried any funny business in all the years they'd been working together. And that was a lot of years, now that he started to think about it. Maybe more than a decade, come to really consider it. They were practically like family at this point, and the one thing family doesn't do (unless you were Lee's family, that was) was turn on each other.

The police car's wet taillights began to fade, although a pair of new sirens were swelling through the night to fill up the void as it sped away. Lee stepped out from behind the dumpster and started running again. A lazy guy would have jogged or walked, he figured, and tried to convince himself that blending in would be a good strategy. But Lee wasn't lazy, and he knew he had to run like hell and keep running until he got to Asylum Avenue. If he could get there...

He wasn't sure. Portland didn't always tell you things like that. Sometimes it'd just give you a hint of an idea and Lee knew it was a good idea to give it what it wanted or else it might give you something you *didn't* want. Run that idea down until you'd given the city—which was more like a girl than a boy, and more like a woman than a man— exactly what it wanted. And then you'd be able to breathe a little bit better, then you'd be able to see a little bit better, then you'd be able to feel that you were cold and wet and hear the rain coming down and maybe even the thunder in the distance, which was totally drowned out by the sirens screeching like some cats from hell.

A different man would have been caught on the spot. But he could smell something wrong in the air the moment he pulled up to the spot with Tommy. He was trying to remember as he ran what Tommy had looked like when he handed him the envelope. Guilty? Or did Tommy always look like that? Were his eyes darting left and right like a rat in the corner looking for a bit of cheese but also looking for the cat? Tom and Jerry? Tommy and Lee?

He wasn't sure. When he got out of this—and he was certain he would get out of this, he could smell that, too. Portland wasn't done with him yet, it wasn't nearly done with him yet, and the blood on his hands—or the blood that *was* on his hands—was only part of the reason he could tell. When he got out of this, he was going to pay Tommy a visit. Probably, he'd kill him. Or he'd hug him and kiss him and tell him it was all right. He wasn't sure which.

He leapt into a few more alleys, hid behind a few more dumpsters, laid flat on the ground under an SUV huffing and puffing like a windvane in a hurricane, and finally he was there. First it was U Street, way back in the Civil War times. Then it was Asylum Avenue. Now they wrongly called it Hawthorne Boulevard, but Lee still called it Asylum Avenue because this is the place where the crazy came from, this is the place where the crazies also went, drawn like moths to a flame, dragged like sacks of potatoes sometimes by policemen and men in white coats called doctors, whatever that even meant these days.

He'd shaken the last of the cars still searching for him. He looked at his wrist to check the time—something around 2 AM., he expected, and was surprised to see that somewhere along the way he'd shattered his watch. There was a bit of blood caked into the cracked glass, and some hair. The long black hair did it for him: that was *her* hair. The realization made him giddy and excited and also sad, because nothing at all that he'd planned for her was able to come to fruition now. It'd all been ruined.

It went all right at first, even though that little voice was telling him something was off. Tommy was just where he was supposed to be. It was raining slightly even then, and windy, and the street was empty as it usually was at that time of night. He had on a black raincoat and his truck was pulled into the far end of the parking lot, lights off. Lee had turned his lights off while he was still on the street, and he pulled into the slot across from Tommy and got out without wasting any time.

He always got impatient toward the end. His blood was hot, his head was in a frenzy. He needed the girl. Even knowing it was dangerous, even feeling and smelling that something was off. He couldn't keep himself from getting out of the car, he couldn't stop himself from striding across the parking lot with the envelope of cash clenched in his fist.

He needed the girl. He needed to take her home. He needed to hurt her, hear her scream. It was a desire bigger than his own personal wants and needs, bigger than thirst or hunger or even emotions like loneliness or depression or greed. It was Portland breathing and sighing with relief with each step he took. It was Portland feeling the blood pumping through her veins and knowing it'd be spilled soon, it was Portland, quiet, solemn, waiting to absorb the sounds of her screams.

Sixth sense be damned, Tommy perhaps looking a little off be damned, he saw the crate in the back of the truck and knew he was half a minute away from having her in the back of *his* truck and then he'd be home in a quarter hour and he could have her in the basement within a minute and then they'd be able to begin and Portland would breathe again, Portland would breathe easy knowing he was giving it blood and screams and pain and torture and...

"Business good?" he'd asked politely.

"Well enough." Tommy never talked much, but he smiled a lot. He didn't smile when he replied, though, and that's when Lee knew something was wrong.

A set up? A sting? He stumbled down Hawthorne Street working it over in his head, gritting his teeth and wringing his hands, trying to figure out how it had all gone so damn wrong. Tommy wouldn't have gone to the police on purpose, that much he was certain of. But he did seem off. The longer Lee thought, the surer he was.

He was still breathing heavy from his sprint through the city. He had to have run for half an hour, a couple miles at least. Now he was here on Asylum Avenue and the whole street was put to sleep and so it was almost totally dark. He noticed for the first time just how hard it was raining, and how wet everything was, and how cold he was. He noticed that the sirens had finally faded into oblivion. He noticed, finally, that his hands were shaking and his chest was still heaving and that he couldn't quite get his breath again. He felt like a vacuum that had a hole poked in the bag.

He started pacing down the street, feeling a bit aimless suddenly. The rope that had him round his navel, the rope that pulled him these three or four miles at a breakneck pace, that helped him avoid all the police and told him to bowl that portly man and his girl over, had been severed. It led him here, and then it fell to the ground, lifeless. Portland had him where it wanted him. Now he had to figure out what to do.

He thought of Tommy again and grimaced. The foreign man didn't look surprised when the sirens erupted to life and the tires started shrieking on the damp pavement toward them. His eyes went wide, sure, and he took a step back... but maybe it was just from the look he saw on Lee's face. Maybe that momentary flash of what Lee now thought was fear wasn't fear of the police, but fear of what Lee might do to him.

For his part, he was certain he looked mad as hell. 'Cause the part of him that had known something was up, that part which he pushed down into the cellar like a bad date, hated to be ignored. He'd been told before that when he got real mad, he looked crazy. Tommy probably saw how furious he was and thought he was crazy. Of course Tommy knew he wasn't crazy, Tommy knew him as well as anyone. But still, that's probably what he thought. Even though they were good friends, Lee recognized Tommy might not be certain how he'd react when he had his back to the wall.

Still, he didn't want to mess with Tommy—not then. He had to sate his bloodlust, even with the police baring down on him. The only way to do that was to leap into the back of Tommy's truck, punch through the thin plywood box that kept the girl he'd just purchased—fairly purchased, with real money, as he'd always done—a good, fair deal—and stab her. Of course, that's exactly what he did. The sirens blared, tires squealed, and before the first note had rung to the other end of the street, he was in the truck, his knife was unsheathed, and he was plunging it into her shocked chest.

Once, twice, three times, pumping his hand like a piston. He twisted the knife.

He hated to rush the kill. It felt wrong, mainly because it *was* wrong—a life was worth more than that, so much more than that, especially one that cost him that much money. But—

A flash of movement a good hundred paces down the slick street made Lee jump back to the present and freeze in his tracks. His whole body tensed like a jack-in-the-box. If his bones could have leapt out of his skin, they probably would have. He figured at that point whichever bit still had his brain—the muscle, flesh, and blood or the white bone skeleton—would do its best to run away.

A quarter second was all it took for him to assess the danger. No, not a policeman. A migrant vagabond soaked from head to toe, pulling a little wagon laden with what appeared to be the contents of a residential trash can. He'd seen it a hundred times before, of course. The homeless were to Portland what the blue collar worker was to the Midwest. It wouldn't be the same without them. Perhaps it wouldn't even work without them.

His hand twitched to his belt. His bloody knife was right where it should be. Let Portland have a little more blood, a little more pain. Leave the man in the rain and let the police try to figure *that* out. Let them try to figure out how he escaped from their grasp, let them try to figure out how he ran so far, so fast, and killed again right under their noses.

They wouldn't figure it out. They never could. Sometimes Lee thought they didn't even care, not really. He thought the police in Portland were a bit like an old, tired dog that saw a fox scuttling into the hen house. The thing is, the dog had been sniffing around the hen house himself just a few weeks earlier and one of the old chickens had pecked him on the nose and now he pretty well hated the damn things.

But of course, it was the dogs job to stop the fox. So he ran at it and barked a little, but really, part of him wished he hadn't seen the fox coming. Part of him thought he might lie down facing the other way tomorrow. If the fox came back, maybe he wouldn't see, and that wouldn't really be his fault, would it? The fox is a quiet animal. Hard to hear coming. Hard to see, even, because it's so low to the ground.

The man pulling the wagon shouted something at him.

He didn't hear the words, but the shout reminded him that he wasn't in any danger. He reanimated his frozen body and began walking again. *Slosh, slosh, slosh* as the rain drummed down around them. He looked down and saw that his shoe had ripped. He wiggled his big toe and grinned at how it poked out.

He waved at the homeless man and said, "going to see the show?"

That earned him a cackle. "You bet your ass. Thought I'd bring the whole family." He motioned at his wagon, seeming to imagine he was lugging about a pair of kids and a wife. Or maybe a husband. Lee wasn't someone to judge about something like that. It seemed not to matter much to him.

He decided on the spot not to kill the homeless man. That was a good joke. He liked jokes. "So where are you really going at this hour? Don't you have a dry place somewhere to stay out of the rain?"

He scowled toothlessly. "Used to, before the city started expanding that dump on 55th. Had a nice overhang, quiet corner, no one to bother me. Now?" He scoffed and looked up at the sky, raising his hands like a man in prayer. The handle of his wagon fell noisily to the street and clanged happily.

Lee felt sorry for him. "Are you all alone out here?"

"Sometimes." He gave Lee a longer, more discerning look, as if he were deciding how much he should say. Then he turned the question around. "What about you? You don't look like you belong out here."

"I don't belong out here," Lee agreed. "A bunch of thugs attacked me a few miles back. Was minding my own business, shopping, and they came screaming out from around the corner. A whole pack of them. Nearly got me, too. If I weren't so fast..." he shook his head. "I don't even want to imagine it. The things they'd have done to me."

"Geez," the wet, dirty man said sympathetically. "Well don't you have someone to call? I used to have folks to call, back when I was your age. You can't be more than 30, can you?"

Lee was nearly 40, but he didn't figure there was a point in correcting the older man. "I don't have anyone to call because I don't have any friends." He didn't actually want friends, or need them. Not even now. Portland was taking care of him. He didn't want to be anywhere but right where he was.

The homeless man grunted. "Guess you could come with me. I got a spot not so far from here. Dry place, normally just a couple girls there. They don't bother no one." He put his hands up to his face conspiratorially and stage whispered, "they're lost in the drugs, if you'd know it. Probably won't even know we've come up to stay out of the rain."

Lee almost started laughing. Could it really be this simple? "Okay. Want help pulling your wagon?"

The old man waved the offer away. "This wagon is as much a part of me as my leg. You wouldn't ever ask a man if he wanted help carrying his leg, would you?"

Lee agreed he wouldn't. He was in a great mood suddenly. This was like a confirmation that everything that happened tonight was supposed to happen, and that he was right to listen to the urges, and that Portland had him safely and firmly grasped exactly where he was supposed to be.

They set off away from the old hospital, which was just as well. Lee loved this place, he loved the way it smelled on Hawthorne and he loved the way the people walked—different when they were in this area, although almost none of them would have known it—and he loved the way the air tasted different. But it was also a dark place for him, a place where he couldn't quite stand still or be certain he was safe.

He remembered the shots again, and couldn't even quite be sure if they'd been given to him or someone else. He couldn't even quite be sure he'd ever been in the hospital at all, held down on a gurney, pumped full of chemicals by doctors with wide, jumpy eyes. Was that him, or a little girl that drowned her neighbor in a shallow pool of tepid water? Was that him, or a murderess that took her husband's head off with an axe? Was that him, or…

After a few minutes went by, the homeless man pointed to an overhang along the side of a big brick building. It was unlit, and ran down half the length of an alley into complete darkness. But the overhang was big enough that even with this torrential rain there was no water at the base of the building. There was a curb that picked the ground up from the street, too. So even though it was flooding, none of the water was going that direction. Marvelous!

"It's dark," Lee said conversationally. "Can't barely see more than halfway down there."

"It gets bright when the sun comes up," the old man said, shrugging. "Besides, this way no one can see us. You know how many times someone's robbed me? And with what happened to you earlier tonight, I figured that'd make you comfortable."

Something swelled in him as he stood next to the vagabond and his wagon at the side of the building and looked down into the cave-like alley. "Are the girls down there?"

"They won't bother us if we don't bother them. Are you shy?"

Lee smiled at him widely. It was hard for him to hear, suddenly. The blood started to thrum in his ears. His belly was churning. The girls *were* down there. He could smell them. He could feel them through the pavement in the soles of his shoes.

When Lee didn't reply, the homeless man shrugged and started to walk down the alley. He struggled to pull his wagon up the curb beneath the overhang. After wrestling with it for a moment, he looked back at Lee and waved at him like he was blind.

"A little help?"

Lee looked up at him, like he just then remembered he was there, and saw that he was having some trouble. He obliged, lifting the back of the wagon, which was surprisingly heavy, and then joined him under the eave and on the sidewalk.

"Thanks," he huffed, seeming to notice for the first time that Lee was distracted. It was creepy the way he'd gone from completely present to half unaware. Like someone with dementia or Alzheimer's, only Lee looked way too young for that. He was like a barn door hanging half open in the yard before a big storm.

Lee didn't reply, which he'd half expected.

The homeless man started down the edge of the building and smiled uncertainly as Lee fell into pace next to him. They walked like that into the dark, getting swallowed up by the shadows. The rain kept falling.

Far away, the sound of a lone siren echoed into their nearly deserted corner of the city.

"Do you think they're after those thugs that attacked you?" the homeless man asked guardedly. "Did you get a chance to tell anyone what happened?"

Lee didn't hear a word of this. His heart was beating as hard as when he was sprinting. He felt like one of his ribs was going to burst through his skin. He could barely see, either, now that they'd left the lone streetlight that illuminated the opening of the alley behind them.

The homeless man started to slow. "You all right, buddy?"

Lee noticed that he stopped, and so he did the same. He turned to him again, finally, and realized what he was meant to do. Portland didn't have to tell him. He could just feel it in the air, in the same way he figured folks who've been hit by lightning could feel it a moment before it happened based on some stories he'd read about that kind of thing. They say your hair stands up on end and the air feels electric and everything gets very quiet right before it strikes.

He reached onto his belt and turned his head inquisitively. Now that he was focusing, he could hear again, at least a little. "What's that?"

"I asked if you were all right. Did you hit your head? It's like you can't hear me."

Lee fell on him, then. But he didn't do it in the way he liked to fall on his victims. He drove at him more like a wolf would fall on a little fawn, with a short burst of pure, raw aggression and an immediately fatal blow to the neck with the sharp edge of his knife.

No time for him to scream—just enough time for him to fill his lungs, only to realize his neck was cut so deep he couldn't actually make any noise other than a sick kind of bloody gurgle.

Lee pulled him into his chest even as he was fighting to push him away. He pulled him tight, tight, tighter—hugging him, trying to show him that he loved him, trying to show that it's not personal. It's just Portland, baby. Nothing to do with who they are or where they've come from. He actually liked the guy. Felt a kinship with him.

"Sorry," he whispered as the fight left the homeless man's flailing limbs and he started to sink to the dry patch of street at the edge of the long brick building in the dark alley. "Sorry, brother."

He let him fall gently, laying him down like he'd lay down a baby. Then he stood over him and watched as the blood pumped out of his gashed throat. It wet the miraculously pristine sidewalk in a dark pool, that in this low light, looked not much different than a rain puddle. Lee rather liked the idea of that. The homeless man was just lying down in a rain puddle.

Of course, Portland knew the truth. The barren sidewalk drank up his blood and reveled as the pain faded out of his body and the light left his eyes. The whole city trembled as it felt him die. The air started to vibrate as it realized there was more to come. Lee was like a modern knight sent out by a powerful king on a quest to save the kingdom. Yes, he'd been anointed by a higher power to perform a grand task to set things right again. Things had to be set right before he could put this debacle behind him.

There were other traffickers in the city. If Tommy was gone, or arrested, or turned over to the side of the sick freaks that locked people in cages and kept them there for their whole lives, so be it. He knew of a few guys who could do what Tommy had done for him, maybe one or two of them who would even charge him less money. Maybe it was time for a change.

And if not, there *were* a lot of homeless in Portland. The city itself didn't seem to mind where the pain and screams came from, not so far as he could tell. His goal, handed down from a great height, he felt, was simple enough. He didn't know of any reason to stop anytime soon. Not with so much going his way.

He stalked down the alley, twirling his knife between his fingers. The homeless man's blood slicked the brick wall. For a second, he thought about the shots again, and the hospital, and the doctors with their chemicals and the way it made you feel crazy and insane and dangerous and violent, and...

Something stirred in the dark ahead of him. A quiet voice whispered something, and then someone groaned sleepily.

So they saw him coming. Good. It'd been a while since he had a proper struggle. The city would revel in the violence.

St. Johns Square *by Igor Beltrame*

Seven Against the World

Johnny looked like a warlord standing in the bed of his brother's pickup truck, looking down at the six of them. At least that's what Ricky thought, then, before everything went to hell. By the end of the few short months that followed, which would change the seven of them forever, he'd think back to that moment and wonder how he ever saw anything but the devil himself. He'd hate himself for the rest of his life for not putting a stop to it then and there. But then, he couldn't have done that—not even if he tried—and he supposed that was really the best part of the story.

They'd been friends since the 1st grade, which is when he moved to the neighborhood and happened to see Johnny playing with his older brother across the street. He wandered over and introduced himself in the way kids did back then, just like his parents taught him. *Hey, my name is Ricky Toez, I'm 7 and I just moved here from Texas.* Johnny said his name was Johnny Walkman and that he was in the 1st grade. His brother had just watched them, not much caring about the little kids. Jack was dead now—run over by a drunk driver while he was on a morning run. Even though he was dead, everyone still called the 1997 Ford Ranger *Johnny's brother's truck*, rather than *Johnny's truck*. That seemed to piss Johnny off sometimes, but what could they do? It was Jack's truck, really, even though Jack was dead. Johnny would have never had the keys to it if Jack were still around. Probably, none of it would have happened at all if Jack were still around. He'd have whacked Johnny so hard across the back of his head that he saw stars for days and that would have been the end of it.

But Jack was dead, and it did all happen. It went a bit like this.

Johnny made a simple declaration. "We're going to make those fuckers pay." He waved his arm and clenched his fist when he cursed, which made the whole thing seem much more serious and dramatic than it really was.

Claire's eyes were about to fall out of her head from how hard she was staring. Ricky had seen girls look at The Beatles like that in old video tapes, but never real people. He kind of understood it though. Although he'd never admit it to a soul—especially not now, after all that awful shit that'd gone down—he thought they were all in love with Johnny in their own way. Girls just loved differently than guys did, unless you were a queer, and then he guessed it was kind of the same. Truth was, he thought any of the guys in the group—Big Ray the football star, Bucking Billy (who famously leapt onto the back of a moose in the 6th grade and rode it halfway down the road), or even Terrance, who was about the straightest laced guy in the entire city, would have dropped down on their knees and sucked Johnny off if he demanded it.

It wasn't always like that, but sometime around the beginning of that year—5 or so months ago, which seemed like years—something had changed. Johnny's acne had cleared up, but it wasn't so plain as that. Sure, he'd been lanky and a little awkward in 9th grade, and now he'd been lifting weights and his chest was filled out and the baby fat had melted off his face and he was handsome rather than *cute*. But still. It wasn't vain, the way everyone was attracted to him.

It was like magnetism. It was like Johnny had found some secret magnet that made people want to be around him and do what he wanted, and even though Ricky had thought about that, and realized it, and wondered at it, he couldn't quite bring himself to fight it. It was just nice to be around Johnny—even when they were doing bad things —because when he smiled at you or told you that you'd done good or asked you to do something and you saw him nod at you, all pleased, it was like getting an *attaboy* from your Dad when you were 5-years-old.

It was like when Grandpa grinned at you and told you that you were a *chip off the old block*. It was like when you got a gold star on your report card from your favorite teacher in the 1st grade.

It felt damn good.

That's the best he'd been able to explain it to the cops and the FBI and the news and his mom and dad and everyone else who'd asked for answers, and that explanation didn't come easy. It took him months to really figure that out, and even when he came upon it, it didn't quite feel right. But he was satisfied with it, mainly because it was the truth—or at least *his* truth. If you asked Claire, she'd have told you something totally different. She'd probably have said that Johnny scared her and turned her on at the same time. She'd probably have said that Johnny made her feel like she didn't have any choice but to do exactly what he asked, she'd probably have said she was afraid he'd hurt her family, or hurt her, or hurt her friends, and so she had no choice but to follow along.

But all that was a load of absolute shit.

The simple truth was, they all wanted to do whatever Johnny wanted them to do. Plain as that. The *why* was the curious part, and the part that even now, Ricky couldn't quite explain. But not being able to explain something didn't make it any less true.

The first of it began just a week or two after school let out. The seven of them were perusing the town and Ricky had the bright idea to ask a guy if he'd go into the liquor store and buy them some vodka. It seemed like, what with how compelling Johnny could be, that the guy might have actually said, "Yes." But he'd looked them over—up to Billy, slightly down to Ray, across to Claire, who was hanging on Johnny's arm, and Kayla, who was hanging on Claire, and then last at Terrance and Ricky. He could still remember the way the guy arched his brows, like he couldn't quite believe it. He almost felt sorry for him.

"No chance, kid. Beat it. Go raid your parents—"

What would he have said? Wine cabinet? Who cares. Johnny caught him with a right hook clean in the jaw, hitting him so hard and so unexpectedly that the big guy—who was a full adult and as tall as Ray—went sprawling back and fell like a cut tree.

Terrance was the only one who spoke up, and he seemed more surprised than upset. "Jesus Johnny!"

Ray started to step forward. He looked like he was about to lean down and check if the guy was alright. But then the store clerk was at the window, gaping at the seven of them like they were part of some gang, and Claire gasped, "*run!*"

Ricky wasn't proud, but he was the first to turn tail. And by the time they were down the street and around the corner, he was laughing his ass off along with the rest of them. It was a great big joke. Johnny smacked the shit out of that goober, knocked his bell off, hit him so hard he cracked his skull on the brick wall of the liquor store and had nosebleeds for weeks. They didn't know that, then, though. They just knew he got him good.

"Asshole should have gotten us some vodka." That's what Johnny said when Kayla asked what he'd hit him for. Like it was math or something. Two plus two is four.

It must have been a few days after that when Johnny's transmission got funky and he came up with a good way to get money. His neighbor a few houses down was going on vacation. The guy collected watches and jewelry; he was always bragging about it and showing it off. Johnny figured they could knock out a window in the back yard and climb inside without anyone hearing. At first, it was just supposed to be the two of them. But then Ray heard, and Ray told Terrance, and Terrance told Kayla because he liked Kayla and of course Kayla told Claire. Someone told Billy—maybe Johnny himself—and before the night came, the whole lot of them were planning to break in.

And that's exactly what they did. Just like Johnny said they should. They waited until a while past midnight, snuck out of their respective homes, hitched rides, rode skateboards and bikes, and then crept through the back yard. Johnny did the honor of breaking the window —somehow quietly—and he climbed through alone. Then he opened the back door, easy as you please, and within an hour they'd amassed a fortune of goods that didn't belong to them which, once pawned, gave them each a couple hundred dollars and paid the mechanic the $1800 necessary to repair the faulty transmission in Johnny's brother's truck.

The cops were called, but no one had a clue as to who committed the theft. Claire and Kayla drove halfway down the coast, all the way to California, to pawn most of their loot—and by the time they got back from the three day trip, Johnny had already planned a new heist.

For his part, Ricky didn't much want to be a career criminal. But Johnny was his best bud. And there was the thing where he'd become more compelling than he should have been to contend with, too. Even thinking back, even knowing everything he knew, he wasn't sure if, given the chance, he could go back and resist him. He thought, sometimes, scarily and frightfully, that if he had that chance, he'd do it all again, exactly the same. Because maybe when Johnny asked you to do something, you didn't actually have a choice. Maybe he wasn't asking at all, or even suggesting, but telling you. Maybe he was a bit like a writer and they were all just characters in his story and he could make them do whatever he wanted just by speaking it into action.

The stealing wasn't the only thing, but the ease with which they were getting away with it seemed to be making everyone feel bolder. After the third house even Ricky had to admit he'd been feeling bullet proof. There was a new pep in all their steps. Ray walked like he was already in the NFL, Billy walked like he'd just hopped on that moose's back yesterday. Claire and Kayla may as well have been models. They didn't walk at all anymore, they strutted.

The day Ricky was thinking about now—when Johnny was standing in the back of his brother's pickup truck and declaring to the six of them that they were going to *make those fuckers pay* was about a month after the first break in. A few folks in the neighborhood had gotten suspicious of them in the way that adults got suspicious of groups of kids who were gathered for no specific reason. A few of them had even made accusations—baseless accusations based on basically nothing other than their raw suspicions that the seven of them looked like they were up to no good.

A few days before that, they were shopping for groceries to have a bonfire at Kayla's house—her parents were gone that weekend—and the cashier had tried to tell a joke to Claire. Johnny didn't appreciate it, and told him as much. He said something like, *was your mother a comedian, or were you just born funny?* Harmless enough depending on your tone and expression, but Johnny wasn't being harmless at all. He must've felt like the guy was trying to flirt. Ricky kind of thought he was just being friendly.

The dude's response may as well have been a slap in the face. "Nah buddy, just winding the clock down. Take a chill pill—or was your mother one of those fancy New York critics?"

Johnny's upper lip curled. That was the only warning. Ricky tensed, though, knowing exactly what was going to happen.

He clocked the guy right in the nose, a good straight right hand that would have sat him down on his butt if the counter and cash register hadn't been behind him. As it were, he just went sprawling back, knocking into the big display and upending cartons of cigarettes and candy and soda bottles. His nose cracked wide open and a big fountain of blood shot out, almost like it was connected to a hose. What a mess! He screamed like a man who'd been confronted with a gun. The manager came beelining out of some office holed away in the back of the store and he had his phone in his hands. His head was shinier and cleaner than a boiled egg, only it was beat red and sweaty.

"I'm calling the police!" he warned.

Johnny looked like he wanted to advance on him. He looked like he'd advance on the whole damn world in that moment. There was something in his eyes—Ricky thought if he actually did have a gun, that he might have actually used it—but then Claire grabbed his arm.

"Let's go!"

Ricky grabbed his other arm, pulling him hard, and he gave up. They sprinted out of the store, still holding various items which they never paid for and never would pay for. Bucking Billy brought up the rear. As they were leaving, he did something which Johnny would never forget.

An old woman was squeezing into the door as they made their mad dash for the exit. Even Johnny slipped past her without bumping her over. Ricky smelled her perfume, which had probably been bottled sometime around the year he was born, and wrinkled his nose as he leapt onto the street.

He looked over his shoulder instinctively. Aside from Billy, he was the last one to leave. That's when he saw the big kid—who was very nearly a man—drop his shoulder into grandma's chest and bowl her over like she was the last pin on your final attempt to break your personal record at the bowling alley.

She let out a breathless squawk and fell hard on her hip. It sounded like something broke, probably because something did break (her leg, her pelvis, and one of her ribs, Ricky later learned). A few people standing about started yelling. Someone up ahead—it sounded like Johnny—howled with laughter.

They ran until their sides were screaming and Claire was falling so far behind they'd have ditched her if they didn't slow. A long ways off, back toward the store, there was a siren blaring.

The store had cameras, of course, and for the first time in all the weeks since they'd been breaking the law, they had some pressure on them. Their blurry, indistinct faces were on the news the following night, and an article was written about the *gang of seven children* in the Sunday paper. It was a bit of a mess, and it made Ricky feel sick to his stomach to read about all the things they were suspected of doing. Amazingly, more than half of the accusations were true. People were pegging them left and right for shit they'd really done! And lots of things they hadn't had a hand in at all, which was almost worse.

An old man called Mr. Darvin that lived at the front of the winding neighborhood Ricky and Johnny called home called a big meeting that most of the old farts who liked to put their nose into kids' business attended. Lots of people seem to have made the connection between the kids in the surveillance footage, the break-ins, the few assaults, and the seven of them always hanging around at Ricky's or Johnny's house. Ricky's own mother even asked him one evening if they'd been up to no good. He denied it all, of course, and she came away nodding. Not because she believed him, but because she *wanted* to believe him. For then, that was enough.

Anyway, Johnny was standing up in the back of his brother's truck and declaring that they were going to make that fucker pay. The old man was the fucker in question.

Normally, he would wind up and begin delivering some kind of impassioned speech. They'd all watch him in various levels of amazement—he was an incredible speaker, a bit like Churchill (or maybe someone else who no one would like to compare him to, really, especially not to his face). This time, though, Johnny didn't wind up at all. He just said that one thing and then looked out at them, as if waiting for someone else to add something in.

Ricky took the chance to ask, "what's the point?"

Johnny's eyes narrowed. "What's the point? The guy is slandering us!"

He looked down at his feet, not wanting to get into an argument, but also not really able to help himself. He wanted to agree with Johnny and make him happy, he wanted to go with the flow and be a positive part of the group. But perhaps for the first time, then, he thought they might be going too far. "Is he, though?"

"Course he is!" Billy crowed in his deep voice.

Ray backed him up with a big furrow in his brow. "My dad told me last night that the kids who were doing all this ought to be strung up and killed. Can you believe that? The whole town wants to kill us just because we broke into a few houses!"

Johnny took back over, then. "They're accusing us of things we *haven't done!*"

It was true. Yet they were also being accused of a lot of shit they *had* done. But Ricky could tell he wasn't going to get through to any of them. Also, there was Johnny, still standing up there and exuding his influence. He wanted to do what Johnny wanted him to do.

"It's not fair," Claire added, as if that weren't obvious. She flipped her hair when she said that, like she was in center frame of an important shot in a movie.

"We need to make them pay," Johnny said again, only this time he wasn't making a statement, he was delivering an order.

Terrance had both his hands in his pockets, and he was leaning back against Johnny's mother's car with an unlit cigarette in his mouth. He talked with his lips never quite parting all the way, so as to keep the cigarette from falling out. "Want me to rough a few people up? Warn them to stop trying to mess with us and get us into trouble?"

"Seems like we have to defend ourselves," Johnny said plainly, as if they were physically under attack.

And that was it. Ricky thought back to it—the way Johnny smiled slightly when he said that, but how his eyes were hard and humorless. The way Claire and Kayla were nodding religiously, the way Ray and Billy clapped each other on the back, like they were getting ready for a football game. Terrance was just leaning on the car with the cigarette between his lips.

He couldn't remember what he'd been doing. Did he smile? Did he nod along with the rest of them? He couldn't even remember if he spoke. All he knew now, looking back, is that whatever he did, it was the wrong damn thing. It was a mistake that cost him more than he cared to think about. In fact, if he harped on it too much, it was bound to drive him crazy.

Terrance straightened up and lit his cigarette. Then he asked, "So what are we gonna do?"

"We're going to kill them," Johnny said lowly. "And we're going to start with that old shit Mr. Darvin."

Johnny got the gun from his brother's room. At least that's what he told the six of them when he pulled it out that evening at St. John's Square. It was late, and they were all lounging beneath the clock, so close they could hear it ticking happily. The moment Johnny produced the weapon, Billy and Ray took to gushing like schoolgirls. The lamplight flashed on the polished barrel. It almost made the gun seem like it was winking. It wasn't an inanimate object in Johnny's hand, but an 8th member of their group, a live and jovial creature which wanted to hang out and have fun and maybe *bang, bang* until they were all laughing like crazy.

The actual schoolgirls gaped, open-mouthed, like Johnny had revealed a strange and rare amulet which might be capable of transmuting a base metal into gold. He may as well have been a magician, or better yet, a wizard performing real magic.

No one asked if Johnny was serious, or if he really meant to use it.

They all knew that he was deadly serious, as serious as a heart attack, as serious as a loaded handgun in a 16-year-old's hands, as serious as anything. He was going to use that gun to shoot Mr. Darvin, probably shoot him right in the face on his front porch, and if someone had the misfortune to see it happen, he'd kill them too.

Or they would. That was a weird thing to think about, but Ricky saw it all while he was staring quietly at Johnny and his gun, he saw it all like he'd never see much of anything ever again. Do anything to protect him. Maybe not even to protect him, but just to please him. Maybe not even to please him, but just for the chance to impress him.

"Where are you going to shoot him?" Terrance asked.

"At his house," Claire said snippily, like it was a dumb question.

"I mean where *at*," Terrance croaked. "Chest? Head? Belly? Do you want to make him hurt? Or just kill him dead, right there, *bam*?"

Johnny shook his head patiently. "I'm not going to kill him you dolt. Claire is."

They all looked to Claire when Johnny said that. She looked as surprised as any of them.

"Me?"

"Of course, sweetheart." He lofted the gun toward her and she drew back slightly. "Are you afraid?"

She shook her head and steeled her expression. "No." She took the gun from him, then, holding it daintily at first, then regripping it and wielding it a bit like an actual person who'd held a gun before. "I'm not afraid."

"Good." He nodded up, toward the clock. They were all alone outside—whether by providence or just dumb luck. "Point it there. Lift it up like you want to use it."

Claire took a few steps forward and lifted the gun, pointing it right into the center of the clock. Anyone could have come along and seen them, then, and called the cops. Maybe that would have been better. But no one did.

Johnny walked up to her and put his arms around her. He lifted her hand a little, making it so it would likely have been level with a grown man's face. "Do you like how that feels?"

She was breathless. "Yes."

"Good. Now pull the trigger. It's not loaded, don't worry. Just practice."

There was a beat of quiet while Claire considered. Then she pulled the trigger and the gun exploded with a raucous, fiery roar of pleasure. The moment it did, the clock itself erupted into a billion splintered pieces of grating metal and flying wood. The immediate, wild destruction seemed impossible. How could one bullet obliterate such a large thing so totally?

Claire screamed—Ricky screamed, too, and so did Ray. The echo of the gun went wide into the city, echoing down the road and against the buildings and way up into the cloudy sky. It probably echoed for miles. Half the city probably woke up from the sound of it.

Claire turned on Johnny, cheeks red, as half of them began to scramble out of the square. "You said it wasn't loaded!"

Johnny just stared at her solemnly. He didn't run at all, he just stood there with his arms crossed. "Always assume a gun is loaded, Love. That's firearm safety 101."

A few days later, Ricky was eating dinner with his folks. His mom had slaved that night, making meatloaf and potatoes and macaroni and fresh rolls and a pie for dessert. There was no good reason for it, she just wanted to make a big dinner to make them all happy. He'd been finishing up the last of the feast on his plate and was turning his mind toward the pie when the phone rang.

Mom got up from the table to grab it. She said, "hello," cheerily, but her face fell almost at once.

"You can't be serious. Are you sure? Oh my God!"

Ricky's stomach went cold, which was a hard thing considering all the warm food inside it. He couldn't hear a peep from the other end of the line, but somehow he knew exactly what his Mom had been told.

"Is he…"

The caller said something quickly and his mother groaned.

"Oh God."

The caller said something else. This time, Mom listened for a while.

Then she nodded soberly.

"Okay. All right. Thanks for letting us know."

Dad was up from the table by this point, and as Mom hung up the phone, he started in on her.

"What's going on?"

"Mr. Darvin was killed tonight." She looked at Ricky and shook her head sadly. "Someone shot him through the heart. Right on his front steps." She tried to say something more and started choking up instead.

Ricky looked down into his plate, contemplating the emotion in his mother's voice. To his knowledge, she hadn't been friends with Mr. Darvin, or even liked him that much. He looked up at his father and was surprised to see a tear in the edge of his eye, and a huge grimace on his normally cheerful face.

"How long ago did it happen? Do the police have any leads?"

She shook her head. "Maybe an hour ago. That was Mrs. Peterson—she said she heard the shot. The police are still there."

Ricky didn't remember choosing to speak. The question just came out. "Do they know who did it?"

"They have no idea," his mother said numbly. "But I bet we all know who did it, don't we?" She looked at his father darkly. "That gang of kids."

His father nodded after a moment to think. "They're graduating to harder crime. Seen it a hundred times. Jesus, and Mr. Darvin was leading the charge against them. Of course it was them."

"Heartless monsters," his mother said, and then she started really crying, and Dad got up from the table to hug her.

Ricky sat there at the table, alone, staring into his plate. For the first time since the summer began, he truly felt guilty and wrong. Hearing his mother sob—stronger now, building—and his father muttering to her—he felt like he'd done something demonstrably wrong.

But of course, he hadn't done anything at all, had he? Other than stand idly by, other than not raise his voice in defiance, other than not warn anyone what Johnny and Claire and the rest of them were planning, other than go along with every awful scheme Johnny came up with, only encouraging them all to do bad things, only...

He stood up abruptly. The power of his mother's crying was somehow strong enough to shake Johnny's influence on him, which waned with distance, and he managed to yelp out a single sentence, which, once uttered, would end all his friendships and several young futures forever.

"It was Johnny and Claire; I knew they were going to do it and I didn't stop them. I'm so sorry, Mom, I'm—" but he couldn't quite state just what he was, because just then, a violent and hysterical wave of sobs came over him.

The rest, as they say, is history. After all the chips fell, Claire received life without parole. The rest of them received markedly lesser sentences, the worst of which was Billy's, two years in the federal penitentiary, and the least of which was Kayla's, which was a single year in a low security women's prison.

Ricky himself served a bit over a year on a sentence of two, and the whole time he was there in prison, he felt like he deserved worse. He wrote like mad while he was there, and read, and finished up high school—doing several years' worth of schoolwork and passing all the tests in just a bit under 9 months.

Mysteriously—or not mysterious at all, the longer Ricky thought about it and the surer he became that the influence was more than just charisma, but a primordial and powerful magic—Johnny escaped scot-free. No probation, no jail time, nothing. He lawyered up, plead not guilty in court, (a tactic none of the others, who admitted their guilt wholesale, dared to consider) and somehow won free.

The day Ricky got out he moved to Boston. He figured Boston was just about as far away from Portland as you could get. Even though he hadn't heard from Johnny once since that night at the dinner table when he admitted it all and threw them all under the bus, even though they were thousands and thousands of miles away from each other, he could still feel his influence tickling away at the back of his mind. He could still remember the way it felt when Johnny turned his gaze on you and told you that you ought to go rob someone or knock them down or maybe even murder them on their front porch.

He felt certain that if Johnny ever got wind of where he was and came to knock on the door of his dorm at Emerson College, he'd have fallen to his knees and done whatever he asked.

PDX Invasion *by Igor Beltrame*

Otherworldly

I'll tell you this much: the world isn't ready for the truth about what's waiting for us in that deep beyond we call *space*. Looking up, up, up into the stars late at night, far enough away from Portland to escape the light pollution, and you'll just about be able to feel it. I mean that, even if you aren't sure at all what it really is. Just look up into the stars. Sit real quiet and look at them. If you get just relaxed enough, you can hear their ships humming. Or maybe it's a feeling, like laying your hand on the hood of a car. Even a deaf guy can hear what that feels like, right? Even a deaf guy can lay his head on a train track and *hear that train a comin'*, even if they aint seen the sunshine since, they don't know when.

They'll kill me for making this public, but the truth is, I'm ready to go. Cancer has near blown straight through my bowels, and I lived a long one, anyway. Back in the 80's when this shit was just starting to go down and I'd barely pinned my wings onto my flight suit, I'd have never imagined I would be breaking rank like this and spilling the beans. But things look a lot different after some time has passed, I've noticed. The older I get, the weirder things seem. Back then it was all *yes sir* this and *no sir* that. They told me to jump and I didn't ask how high, I flew.

And I saw shit I wasn't supposed to see. Most of us in Oregon did. Got to the point where, what, with reporting it all on recorded voice communications and those communications being stored away at some federal base, they had to do something. What were we supposed to do but call it out on the radio when we saw something that wasn't supposed to be there? Of course, everyone was mighty interested in what was going on, too. The boys and girls in the towers were as intrigued as we were, maybe more so, because they'd been seeing it for years. Most of the time when they called it out to whoever was in the air, the guy wouldn't be able to spot anything. But there was a few of us who were damn good at it.

First time I ever saw anything worth talking about I was flying over the coast in an F-20 Tigershark, which remains to this day my favorite ride. Radar was clean as a whistle, and my visuals were clear for miles. Could just about see to the ends of the Earth, it felt like. No clouds in the sky. Perfect flying conditions.

Ashamed to admit it, but ground actually called up to me before I spotted it myself. They said something like, *confirm visual at your 6. You see something up there?* I asked, *what's the elevation?* While I craned my neck around to see what they were talking about. *6800 cruising altitude, speed TBD, there's some kind of interference on it.*

And then I *did* see it, probably about half a mile out from where I was at. I spun about like a top—the Tigershark was no slouch, let me tell you, there was barely a quicker jet in all the world at that point. I put it through its paces, then, just because I had an excuse to really turn it up.

Hard to tell, I'd told them as I picked up speed. My best analysis, being so far and moving so fast, was that I was looking at some kind of silver balloon. But it was a bit big, and they'd suggested it was moving. *What are you marking it as?*

We aren't marking it as anything, they'd replied. Then they added that all so sweet line, a phrase I'll never forget. *UFO until you identify, Major. UFO.*

I got up well over 1000 MPH, probably close to top speed, which was officially 1500. I definitely felt it, too, but not so much that it made my head funny. Half a mile out, I should have closed the distance on the balloon in a snap. Literally.

But it didn't get closer.

Jesus, ground had said. *You're cooking. But it's cooking too. What the hell is it, Major? Can you see it?*

I can see it all right, I'd said, cursing. *It's fucking tracking me. You guys getting this? It's not getting a lick closer or further away. Looks like a freaking balloon, but it's got to be a plane.*

A silver balloon? Ground had said snappily, like they already knew. *That's right.*

I chased it all the way down the coast to California before they called me back. Ended up landing at another base, had to do about a dozen debriefs, signed a bunch of bullshit NDA's and top-secret clearance nonsense stuff. Made a few oaths, I don't remember most of it.

By the end of that year, I guess it was 1981, I'd had at least a dozen more encounters with the bastards. Always looked the same, big silver balloon things, and always kept about a half mile away. No matter how fast we went—I heard of some boys in Blackbirds even that couldn't come close to catching them—they tracked us to stay just so far away as to not let us see them. I heard of a rookie once that launched a freaking missile at them, no shit. Launched a damn missile over the entire continent, and he didn't even get discharged. Just a stern talking to and no flying for a few weeks.

By 1982, it was clear to everyone in the squadron that these guys liked me. Not sure why, but they appeared during my flights, and tracked me, about triple as much as the next guy, who was at least triple as the third. Most only had one or two encounters. I had well over thirty.

Got pressed into joining some kind of UFO study that the military had going on. They used me like bait and the ships showed up enough that they kept using me well into the late 80's. By that point, I'd been doing a damn good bit of research myself. I was asking questions that were getting me into trouble sometimes, poking around places I shouldn't have been, asking for lots of favors and making lots of calls to people that sometimes weren't too happy to talk to me once I began asking questions.

I guess the first time I really decided I wanted to find out what was happening was near 1990, after a few years of being plagued by these sons of bitches and not much liking it the more I thought about it. We were Air Force, and I'll tell you what, none of us quite liked to know that there was some foreign craft up there that could run circles around us. Made us feel funny.

I'd told my wife all about it. She's the only one I ever told that I knew in my private life, at least up to the point that I publish this. My point is, she knew what was going on over Portland, and had been doing some research of her own on the sly. She was a lawyer and a private investigator, so she could really turn things up.

Must have been in late '89, sometime in December if I recall right, when I came home and she asked me, "Honey, do you know Portland has more UFO sightings than any place in the world?"

That took me off guard. I laughed. "Well I'm not surprised to know it. Are they keeping tally of my encounters? I hope you haven't been reporting them to the public."

She'd laughed. Of course not, she said. "But don't you think that's peculiar?"

I did. I'd been flying a few years before being stationed in Portland, and never seen anything like what was happening out here. Never heard of anyone else who had, either. It was damn weird, for sure.

"I'm thinking of doing an investigation," she said.

I tried to put the brakes on her at once. But something about Milly, if she got her mind into something, the damn President himself wouldn't have been able to stop her. "Now you'll go and get me into trouble. Maybe yourself, too."

"I'll keep it quiet." She promised.

And she did. I warned her not to mess with it, and she told me she'd be careful, and that was just about the end of it, far as I knew. Until a few months later, she asked if I'd be willing to meet someone from work with her.

I told her I was flying the next two nights, which was true. The UFO studies were morphing into a night thing—the contact rate was considerably higher at night, especially when the moon was thin or gone altogether. We gathered the crafts were a bit shy, in other words, and didn't like to be out in the day. Which was just as well, with NVG's we could see them fine, and radar didn't miss them much except for when they'd really rocket up their speed. They went so fast they might as well have fully disappeared, you see.

Anyway, I told her it'd have to wait for the weekend. Fine, she'd said. The weekend is great.

Weekend came around and we went out to a bar. Halfway there I asked, hey, who is this fellow anyway? *He's someone I met during the investigation* she'd said, all nonchalant.

The investigation? I'd asked, a little miffed.

That's right. She tried to say it like it was no big deal.

Maybe it wasn't a big deal. It felt to me, driving to the bar late at night, that this shit was top secret. I'd really get into trouble—real trouble—if they found out I'd told my wife and she was running around talking to people about UFO's. The suits that were heading this project weren't military, alright? I never quite could confirm who they were, CIA or FBI or some deep state organization with no name because it's too damn secret even for that.

Like I said, Milly didn't mess around. She set her mind and that was that. I knew enough not to fight her too hard, though. So I went to the damn bar and wouldn't you know, that was the tip of the 'berg, as they say. Sometimes I think about that night—and I think about Milly, who I like to imagine is up there in the stars—and I wonder if it was all worth it. I know more than just about any human on Earth about this stuff, and it all began there in the bar with a short, diminutive man who introduced himself as Nigel.

Nigel had a bunch of acne scars on his face, and a nose that was about two times too large, which made his eyes and mouth seem comically small. If a name like Nigel wasn't enough, he had red hair, too, which I've found to be the least fortunate hair color for a man. I studied him for a long time in the low light of the bar when we first got there. Milly ordered us drinks, and Nigel got to talking, and pretty soon I learned what this was all about.

Nigel was a conspiracy theorist, an alien hunter, a recorder of what he called "unexplainable phenomena." He had a briefcase with him, and as if to prove to me that it wasn't empty, he opened it up before any of us had so much as finished our first round of drinks, and he was pushing highly classified documents at me and signed confessions at me and some foreign stuff from China and Russia and Germany. All of it pertained to UFO's and alien encounters.

The most interesting shit he had was from right here in Portland, though. Presidential writings, a collection of reports from private citizens, and, what I think was the biggest and best collection of information, a great big glob of stolen documents from a private chemical company that'd been under investigation for dumping their toxic waste into the Willamette since the turn of the 20th century. I won't name the company, just because I've still got a slight hope that I'll be allowed to live out my life in peace, but I reckon anyone who cares would be able to find the name of them in about half an hour of searching on the internet.

One drink turned into two, and half an hour turned into a couple. Before we knew it, the barkeep was shouting for last call and we were just about the only people in the bar. Nigel was as forthcoming as a guy who thought he was talking to someone that was going to break it all open for him would be expected to be. He wasn't holding anything back. I studied the documents as long as I wanted, I hummed as he tried to get stuff out of me, and nodded politely, interestedly, as he told me every damn thing he'd ever learned or known.

What he wanted from me was knowledge. He thought I knew more than I really did. I think Milly thought I knew more than I really did, too. By remaining vague and a bit mysterious, I think I kept him thinking that for a lot longer than was fair. But I did confirm for him that the military here knew without a doubt about the UFOs, and that we were actively studying them and tracking them to the best of our ability. That seemed to make him real happy. He was thrilled to know I'd had so many personal encounters. I guess a guy like that begins to feel a little crazy, and every time he talks to someone who has their laces straight and their tie on right, well, he feels a little less like a lunatic.

We left the bar and stood at the bed of my truck for a bit, still shooting the breeze. I think Nigel was telling me about his organization, trying to get me to join or at least promise to show up to one of his meetings, which I never did do and never had any plans to do, when Milly finally interrupted us.

She'd been pretty quiet up 'til then, but it seemed like she'd lost patience. "Nigel, are you going to tell him what you told me?"

The little guy squirmed a bit when she said that. "I told you that was--"

"And I told you that my husband wasn't just some robot suit," she interrupted. "I told him I'd bring him so you could meet him and see he was the real deal."

Nigel looked me up and down, then, like he was really trying to tell what kind of guy I was.

"What's this all about?" I felt a bit like they'd been holding back on me, and didn't appreciate it.

"We've had a breakthrough," Nigel confessed, possibly a little drunkenly. He wasn't slurring his words, but his cheeks were bright red and he wasn't fully steady on his feet.

The parking lot was deserted, and the only light to see by was from a flickering lamppost about fifty paces away. I couldn't quite tell in that low light whether he was smirking or grimacing. "A breakthrough?"

"They've found something," Milly said eagerly. She grabbed onto my arm and her grip was so tight I couldn't tell if she was scared or excited. It put me on edge.

I looked at Nigel seriously. "Well?"

"They're here," he'd said, all wide eyed and furtive. "*Right here in Portland.*"

I probably looked stupid, staring at him all confused. "Yeah?" We'd been talking about it all night, you know, all the stuff I've said here. Guys in my squadron back on the east coast had never heard a thing about UFO's, I'd never seen anything unexplainable before Portland, the investigation was taking place here specifically *because* the sightings were far more common here.

"The aliens are right here in Portland," he explained patiently, whispering like someone was listening in on us. "Right under our feet."

That got my attention. I could tell he didn't just mean UFO's; I'd heard plenty to tell me just what this guy believed. "Literally?"

"Literally," he said calmly. "There's something in Forest Park for sure, they use it as a base. And there's something underneath the Willamette, just a bit north of here. And..." he lowered his voice so much I had to learn in to hear "...you ever heard of the Shanghai tunnels?"

I had, actually, because of this old article from a magazine I'd picked up on base when I first moved to Portland. The Shanghai Tunnels were kind of like the Paris Catacombs. A bunch of sailors and unscrupulous type used them during the 19th century to funnel slaves and stolen goods. Far as I knew, they'd been all closed up and weren't used anymore.

"You're trying to tell me there are aliens inside this city right now? On the ground? Not inside their ships?" I looked at Milly, suddenly feeling like she might be pulling a prank of epic proportions on me. "You believe this?"

She told me she did, real earnestly.

I gave Nigel my best *I mean serious business* look and asked him a question I wish, now, I could take back. "Can you prove any of it?"

"They're dangerous," he said. "More dangerous than you can imagine. There's a reason the government is studying them. It's not because they're curious. *It's because they're scared.*"

"Can you prove it?"

He thought about it for a long time. Then he nodded. "Yeah, I guess I can. If you give me some time to get things together."

On the way home, Milly asked if I thought she was crazy. "Sort of," I'd said. Then I laughed and told her I thought I was crazy, too. That got us both to giggling, and believe it or not, that was the end of the conversation that night. She let it rest a few days, and I appreciated that, 'cause at work nothing slowed down at all. I kept flying patterns, they kept watching, occasionally the UFOs would appear. I'd give chase, they'd track me at a precise and steady distance and speed until they got bored and disappeared.

These things started to seem more ominous after Nigel's warning that the aliens were dangerous. The idea of them living on the ground in Portland was completely fantastical, and totally impossible, but the more I thought about it, the more sense it made. Especially with all the junk he'd shown me from other countries. There were a lot of them on Earth if even half of it was true.

A few weeks later, Milly said we should talk about it all. We went out for a drive, turned up the radio, and did just that. The radio was in case we were bugged. It was easy to talk over it after a while, and safer than talking at home.

"Nigel hasn't been picking up his phone. I've left messages. Dropped by his place. Called the paper where he works. I think something's happened to him."

I hadn't been expecting that, so it took me a minute to digest.

Milly wasn't feeling patient. "Hello?" she prodded.

"Well, he must have gotten picked up by the feds," I'd said. "Are you sure he isn't just sick or visiting family or something?"

"How can I be sure?"

Fair enough, I told her. "How long has he been missing? When's the last time you spoke?"

"Last Friday."

So seven days. He'd been MIA for seven days. Too long for a stomach bug, too long to have not returned calls. "And his work hasn't seen him?"

"Nope."

A little fear snaked down the back of my neck at the thought of Nigel having gone too far. The military or FBI or CIA or whoever was involved in all this might have gotten to him. How long would it take for him to point the finger at Milly? Then they'd know I talked, they'd know everything, and I'd lose my job and probably get put in prison.

Things weren't looking good. "He was trying to gather proof, huh? That's what he'd been doing, right?"

"Maybe he did," Milly breathed heavily. I'll never forget how worried she sounded, and how consumed. This was the biggest story any investigator had ever delved into, so far as I was concerned. It made Watergate look like a page nine tabloid article. The magnitude of it was so tremendous, I think neither one of us ever actually wanted to talk about it. Aliens living amongst us in the 20th century, all over the world, the military knowing about it—blowing the lid on a story like that would cement you as the greatest journalist in history.

Milly was dedicated not just because it was a big story, though. She was dedicated because the public deserved to know. That's what I've realized, finally, after all these years. The public deserves to know about this.

"He was gathering footage. I guess one of the places they move around is Forest Park, and so he had video cameras and other things out there. I don't know where he was storing it all. But..."

I flashed back to that night in the parking lot at the bar. "He said they were dangerous. Do you think...?"

Milly shuddered. "I don't want to think about that."

I scoffed at what that meant. "So now we're *hoping* the FBI or CIA or military picked him up?"

The humor wasn't lost on her. "I guess so," she laughed, too.

We kept driving for a bit, each thinking, and finally I came out with the big question. "So, what are we going to do?"

"I don't know what we can do," she said.

"Give it up?" I offered hopefully, knowing there was no chance of that. Once Milly tasted blood, that was it. She was like a shark. It wasn't going to end in anything but success or extravagant failure.

She didn't even acknowledge that as an option. "We have to get proof of our own. And you're going to have to go on record once we do."

I didn't have any desire to throw my career away for this story, but I wasn't going to tell her that. "How can we get proof?"

"We'd need a body, or some convincing footage." She thought about it, humming a little as I drove down the dark street—we'd traveled far into North Portland at that point. "A body would be best."

"You really think they're little grey guys?"

"That's what all the witnesses have said." She shrugged, not seeming to care. "They're made of flesh, and they can die. At least it appears that way. We could kill one with a gun."

I thought about that. Would it be illegal to kill an alien? It seemed like it should be. "They're dangerous, though. That's what Nigel said."

"We're dangerous, too." Milly smiled at me, kind of in a silly way. "Right?"

She had no idea how right she was. Humans were the most dangerous animal on the planet, at least aside from these aliens, maybe. "So, we're going to just go hunting?"

Milly sighed. "Do you have a better idea?"

I shook my head. "Aside from dropping this whole thing once and for all?"

She bared her teeth at me, like a dog. "I won't do that."

"We don't know what happened to Nigel," I reminded her. "He could be dead. Do you realize that?" I didn't personally believe it, then. I thought for sure he'd been taken in by some agency or another. But I did recognize it was possible.

Milly seemed to be more afraid of that than I was. "I know." She gulped. "That's why we have to keep going. That man dedicated a decade of his life to this. And folks here—folks who are supposed to be with us—" she motioned angrily, and I knew she was talking about the military and the government "-they aren't even telling the public the bare minimum."

She wasn't wrong. I was about to reply to her when I realized, with a severe start, that I'd drove clear across town, over two bridge, through a nice residential neighborhood, and had found myself at the edge of Forest Park. The place Nigel mentioned was one of their bases of operation.

I hit the brakes and Milly jerked against her seat belt. "Damn!"

I whipped the car onto the side of the street and put it in park. The trees of Forest Park were looming just before us. It was dark ahead, so dark you could barely see. "Do you realize where we are?"

She looked about, and then paled. "Why did you go *here*?"

I laughed at her, a little meanly. "Don't you want to go hunt them?" It felt damn creepy to me to be out there. I was guessing Milly felt the same.

She hit my shoulder to show she was serious. "I want to get the hell out of here. Let's go home."

"Fine," I told her. We'll go home. And we did. Only this time, all the drive, we didn't much talk at all. I tried to remember thinking about Forest Park or making the conscious decision to drive there. The thing was, I couldn't. I wouldn't have gone there for the life of me. Not without a gun, and I didn't drive around with one of those back then.

"Why'd you go there?" Milly asked when we pulled back into our own neighborhood. Maybe, by then, the shock of it was starting to wear off on her.

"I don't rightly know," I said, as sincerely and seriously as I could. "I mean it. I realized it just as sudden as you. Was like something made the car go that way. The more I think..." I shook my head and kind of chuckled, even though my whole body was wracked in goose bumps "...I don't remember making a single turn or touching the gas pedal the whole damn way there."

Milly didn't say anything to that. We got out of the car and went inside. I locked the doors, which wasn't an every night sort of thing in those days, 'cause we lived in a nice community, a gated place with well-to-do people. It was around 9:30 when we went to bed. I kissed Milly good night—she'd put on a face mask and looked a bit like a horror show, but I still thought she was beautiful.

She kissed me back. We both laid back and contemplated things for a while, silently, each wondering if the other was asleep I bet. I think I finally drifted off about an hour later.

When I woke up again, it was bright as day inside the house, and there was a horrible whirling noise that sounded like a kind of futuristic turbine filling up the world. It could have been a mechanical tornado, or the inside of an industrial washing machine on Mars, or... the steady, revolutionary thrum of an interplanetary ship's engine.

The first thought I had, weird as it is to admit, was *that's going to wake the neighbors*! Made me feel guilty. Then I looked for Milly—my hand shot out onto her side of the bed and my searching fingers landed on empty space.

That got me out of bed, blinking and trying to shield my eyes from the light so I could see—but it wasn't coming from just one place. It was streaming in through the windows, sure, but it was also coming in from the ceiling, and from the walls, and from the damn carpet. It was like being *inside* the sun. Fortunately, it wasn't hot. Just loud.

I started stumbling and feeling my way down the hall. I called out for Milly desperately, loud as I could, but I could barely hear the noise of my own voice, let alone hope someone else could. I bounced down the walls clumsily and eventually landed in the living room, which was where I wanted to be. I headed for the front door. I thought I knew exactly what these bastards were trying to do. They were going to take Milly from me.

The whole thing lasted a minute, but I'm certain my heart beat a whole year's worth of blood through my body. I could barely breathe or think, I couldn't see at all, I couldn't hear at all. I was more afraid and angrier than I'd ever been. By the time I wrenched the door open, I realized I didn't have a gun, but there was no time to go back.

I called for her again, *"Milly!"* and there was no reply, only the louder and somehow more blinding noise and light.

Then there was a weird *pop*, just as I got to the porch steps, and everything cut off all at once. The light and noise, the confusion and pain in my head, it all cut off and I was standing in my boxers on the porch, late at night, feeling damn cold.

I wanted to scream for Milly again, one more time, and was about to when my head got light and I realized I was going to faint.

Woke up in the morning all alone in bed, fully dressed with my shoes on. Every light in the house was on, all the televisions were on, the oven and microwave were on (with nothing inside), the baths were running full blast, as were the sinks, the thermostat was cranked to 85 degrees, and...

Milly was gone. Milly was gone and I knew what'd happened, I knew exactly what'd happened and I cried like a damn banshee while I ran around turning all the crazy shit off. It was just a bit past 8 AM, and judging by the lack of camera crews and police sirens I knew at once that somehow, no one in the neighborhood had heard the raucous.

I felt it in my gut that they'd taken her, but I called for her and searched for her anyway. There was no sign of a break in, no notes that she'd left, the car was still in the driveway, her things were still there, even her purse. She hadn't left. She'd been taken.

I kept a top on it for a while at work, but eventually the pressure got to me and I cracked like an egg. Got a medical discharge a few months later and was out on my ass like a villain, with not much retirement money to keep me afloat, and not a soul in the world I felt like I could talk to.

I've kept my trap shut until now mainly because I'm a coward and I was so goddamned scared I couldn't sit up straight. But along with that fear there's always been the anger, and finally, here recently, the sense that I've been failing Milly and failing her memory. Portland deserves to know what's around here—America deserves to know, hell, the whole world deserves to know.

This is Major Billy T. Beck of the United States Air Force, and I swear on God and country that the above story is true. I give you my word as a man and widower. Do with this what you will.

Cursed by Sergey Shiribokov

THREADER

T hreader rolls out of bed a few minutes past 7:00 and finds a note scrawled on the windowpane next to his nightstand. The writing is thin and oddly styled. Some of the letters seem out of place, or even just wrong. Still, he can make sense of it. He's gotten good at interpreting their curious scrawl. Reading it puts a chill on the back of his neck. He can almost feel the long nail that scratched into the glass running up his spine. He can almost hear it.

It's a simple message. *We require food.* Beneath that, in cleaner script: *Kill the GIRLS.* Threader has never seen the demons, but he's never seen the wind, either, and he knows it exists just the same. When the wind blows, leaves tumble and branches bend and bits of trash from the dumpster behind the diner whip out and run amok in the dirty streets. You can't see the wind gripping the trash, you can't see the wind pulling it out from the trash can, you can't see it dragging the branches down like a little boy hanging from the end of it. But you know it's the wind.

His father called them aliens, but to Threader, they always seemed like demons. Not come from another planet, but come from *this* planet, deep within the Earth. Not extraterrestrial but Biblical, or at least magical. 'Course, his father had actually seen them, and communicated back and forth with them, and all Threader has ever been able to do is hear them and read their notes and witness the spectacular things they're capable of doing when given proper fuel.

And he's been able to feel them, of course. He's felt them working at his body and his mind. He's felt their strength and their power coursing through his veins.

They truly do exist. He's always known if he was to tell someone—anyone—about what was going on that they'd throw him into the nut house. Or if they found out even a small bit about all he's done for them, they'd throw him in prison. He thinks he'd rather be in prison than in the crazy house. His father is in prison. Maybe they could be cellmates. Maybe if both of them got put in prison, the demons would let them out. 'Cause he's the last man in the family, and near as he can figure, the demons really like his family. They've been passing down the job for a couple hundred years at least. A dirty job, true, but a good one. It pays well. Not just in money, but in long life and power. His great grandfather lived to be over 110 years old, and was rich all his days.

The demons like kids most of all, but they'll consume the essence of just about any living thing. Threader has a daughter, and he used to have a wife, but she died in a wreck when Bells was five. Bells is 15, now, and beautiful as the sun. He's always felt the one thing he couldn't do was hurt her. But the demons aren't asking that of him. They probably know he can't do that. They're not foolish.

He brushes his teeth and looks at himself in the bathroom mirror. He's lost weight recently. They've been hungry, and demanding more of him. He stole two horses from the back of a travel trailer a few nights ago and brought them all the way out onto the edge of the Willamette where the river meets an empty bank. He thought that'd keep them sated for weeks. But now...

He spits into the sink, washed his mouth out, and wipes his forearm across his face. He looks back into the mirror and studies himself. Sometimes, he thinks they're changing him. His cheekbones are different than they used to be. His nose is differently shaped. The set of his mouth—it didn't used to be so pursed. He looks like an angry librarian.

Most of all, his eyes. They were hazel as a boy. Green in the sun. Light brown inside.

Now they're dark, approaching black.

He leaves the bathroom and is unsurprised to discover Bells is awake and already in the kitchen. It smells like bacon and eggs and—

"Cinnamon rolls!" she trills as he rounds the corner. The oven swings open and proves her point. There's homemade icing on the counter, and the old recipe book from her mother beside it.

"Smells just like I remember," he says fondly.

She grins at him. "I thought I'd butter you up before I asked if Raya and Charlie could come over tonight. We want a girls night."

He's not surprised. The demons make his job as easy as possible. They've got a way of influencing things to work out. They want him to kill the girls; they've made sure the girls are going to come over. "Sure thing."

They eat breakfast and talk for a while before she shoulders her schoolbag and waves goodbye. He stares at the door after she leaves and thinks about what he's going to have to do tonight.

Raya and Charlie are nice girls. But the horses were probably nice horses, too. Once he gets his commands, he tries not to think too much about what he has to do. It'd be like fussing over the forecast on the weather channel, or the presidential election. What the hell is he going to do about a thunderstorm?

What he thinks about are what he calls the sticking points. Murder isn't all that easy, especially not these days. You've got to plan it well. With Bells involved, he's going to have to pull this off without a hitch. He can't risk things going sideways. If she ever found out—prison would be better than that.

But still. Fortune favors the bold. The demons only ask of him what he can deliver. Not a sentiment that's popular with his father, but it feels true to him. They've pushed him hard before, but never over the edge. He always has what it takes to get the job done. And this isn't easy, it's rarely been easy. But he'll make it happen.

He goes back to the window and reads the message again. ***We require food. Kill the GIRLS.*** Not Bells. Lord no. Raya and Charlie are expendable, but not Bells. Surely they know that.

He stages the basement for the kills. It's not hard to kill a couple kids, but he wants it to be clean. All of his gear is in that underground crypt. He keeps the key to the door that leads into his private area hidden in the false bottom of his nightstand. He retrieves it, flicks on the light from inside the pantry, and then opens up the door and scuttles quickly down the steps. It smells like old wood and concrete. He takes a deep, happy breath, and then sets to work.

Laid out on his workbench are all the things he'll need. Hanging up on a peg board are the things he doesn't need, but will use because he wants this to go well. Rope, chains, tape, sharp knives. These were his father's things, as this was his father's house. On the bench is a double bit axe, a shovel, a pair of pliers—and most importantly, in a locked box which he opens using the combination 1337, a smorgasbord of pills and prescriptions that, if mixed properly, could put a troop of elephants to sleep.

There's no need for him to be cruel. He's killed a few people he knows. In all events, he summarily drugged them, dispatched them with clean and efficient cuts to the neck, and delivered them to the drop off destination. Always on the edge of the Willamette.

He thinks they live in the water, or maybe in Forest Park. Probably, they're sprawling all around and inside Portland, maybe underground in those old tunnels, maybe hidden away in dark corners of the city. He's not sure. He doesn't really care. Threader's found it's best not to worry about those kinds of things.

All he really needs are the pills and a sharp knife. He'll drug all three of the girls, even Bells. He doesn't like that part, but there's no avoiding it. There will be hard questions for him after it's done, but none he won't be able to answer. *Food poisoning, you all got so sick—I took the girls to the hospital.* The hospital won't ever get them, of course, and things will get messy. For a while, Bells might even suspect him.

But he won't leave a trace. He won't leave a single trace of his crime. And the bodies will never be found. He won't screw this up. It'll be fine.

He looks at himself in a dusty mirror over the workbench. There's a crack running through the center of it, but he's learned to see past it. He says the mantra aloud: "I'll be fine. It'll all be fine." The man in the mirror seems like he believes it. The longer he looks at the man, the less he feels like he knows him. The demons have changed him. All the things he's done for them over the years. He's not the same man he was when he graduated high school and got a job delivering papers. That fellow wasn't half bad. But the man in the mirror, he—

"It'll all be fine," the man says, staring at him hard. "It'll all be fine."

Bells fiddles with the old journal and looks up at the clock for the third time this period. Raya shoots her a sympathetic glance. Charlie's studying an old article, somehow actually staying on task and doing the class activity. She brushes a mop of black hair off her shoulder, throwing it over her back, and seems to redouble her attention on the article. Bells just watches her.

Raya nudges her elbow. "Second thoughts?"

She checks to make sure Mr. Tapport isn't looking at them. He's reading an old novel, as usual. Tapport doesn't give a damn what they do in class, as long as they don't talk. He's always too busy reading or writing. He's a shitty teacher, but she likes him. He's kind of cute.

"No," she murmurs. And she means it. After finding her grandfather's old journal and reading about their family history—after tailing her dad for the last few weeks and discovering what he's been doing—she's determined. She's been weak all her life, she's been looked over all her life. It's finally time for *her* to get some power. She's going to take her inheritance whether Dad's ready to give it up or not.

Raya's pretty. She has shoulder length blonde hair, full lips, wide blue eyes. Bells thinks she could be a model. Instead, she's focused on cooking and cleaning and wants to find a husband. Her parents are religious. She says she isn't, but the proof is there in her goals. She prays before they eat, and still brings a bible when she sleeps over. Bells doesn't mind, but she's worried it'll make this all harder for her. Killing is pretty much the worst thing to do. Worshiping demons might even be worse. Not that she plans to worship anything.

Raya raises her eyes at her, like she doesn't believe it. "Okay then."

Bells bares her teeth at her. "Okay then."

Finally, Charlie looks up from her article. She's the most confident, somehow. She's seemed simultaneously excited and nonchalant all day. "Hush, you two. We've got this. It's going to be easy."

Bells starts to reply and as the school bell rings, she nearly jumps out of her skin. She hits her knees on the bottom of the desk and bites her tongue so hard it bleeds.

No one notices except Raya and Charlie. The class makes enough noise pushing their desks on the floor and rattling their backpacks to drown out a scream, and all she did was gasp. Her friends are wearing twin expressions of suspicion and concern.

"You don't have the heart, do you?" Raya whispers. She looks at Charlie and sighs. "We're going to have to do all the hard stuff."

"It'll be worth it, even if that's the case." Charlie shoulders her bag and starts for the door without seeing if they'll follow. They do, of course. They always do. Charlie's the one who had the idea in the first place, who found out that Bells' came from a long line of killers, including her grandfather and great grandfather. Charlie's the one who discovered that there was something wrong and dangerous with her father. Charlie was the one who discovered what they might be able to get if they took his place. When Bells actually started looking, it didn't take long to find the journal in the attic, and then it was all confirmed. The last piece of the puzzle was tailing Dad, and that was easy enough. What they'd discovered then turned her stomach over. Somehow, it made her more interested in him, too. But only to a certain point.

Raya grabs Bells' hand and squeezes it. Bells smiles at her warmly. Charlie can be a little rough sometimes. It feels to her like they don't fully appreciate the sacrifice she's making. It's her father, after all. And they aren't even doing it because the monsters asked them to. They're just doing it for power. Because if he disappears, the next in line will be Bells. And Charlie thinks they'll be able to ask for more than her father and grandfather ever asked for. She thinks if they do things right, they'll be able to uncover the truth about who, or what, is pulling the strings behind the scenes. Money and power are great, but sating your curiosity is better.

They pile into Charlie's jeep in the parking lot. The roof and doors are off, it's summertime and sunny out. The light feels amazing on her face. Bells leans back in the backseat and puts her face up to the sky. She puts on her sunglasses and closes her eyes. She can feel her skin warming up.

"He's never going to see this coming," Raya says for the third time that day. "He has no idea we know. He thinks we're coming over just like we've come over a hundred times before."

Bells doesn't reply. She just sits in the backseat, feeling the sun on her skin.

Charlie turns the jeep on and the whole thing starts vibrating. It's seen better days. The tires are bald, the once bright red paint is all faded and worn, and sometimes it does this weird thing when they get on the highway and the whole engine just shuts off. Around town it's pretty good, though. Aside from the shaking. Occasionally, Bells has thought the shaking was rather pleasant, depending on her mood. Other times it feels like someone has grabbed you by the back of the neck and is trying to make your arms and legs fall off.

The wind makes it so talking isn't possible. They've already talked enough as far as Bells is concerned, anyway. There comes a point where plotting a murder, even your own dad's murder, becomes a little tiresome. She's ready to just get on with it.

Charlie turns the radio up. The rest of the way home, the girls listen to the lilting voice of some indie punk singer. The guitar sounds like a wildcat screaming and the drums are like a trio of teenagers beating the hell out of a bandstand. The lead singer sounds like he might be ready to cry or yell. She likes it.

They pull into her driveway and Bells sees Dad in the window. She looks away from him and says to the girls, "just play it cool. Don't give us away."

Threader feels a pang as he's watching the girls hop out of the jeep. For the first time in a long time, he feels a bit annoyed at the demons. What the hell are they having him do this for? Raya and Charlie have been coming around here since they were barely out of diapers. They're Bells' oldest friends. It'll hurt her bad, even if she never knows what happened. Raya and Charlie would never hurt a fly. They're more innocent than any creatures on the planet.

They grab their bags and come running up the steps. He opens the door to let them in and they all greet him at once, airy voices trilling *Dad, Threader, Mr. T* in tandem. Smiles, waves, Raya bows sarcastically and Charlie twirls.

"You mind if we take over the living room tonight, Dad?" Bells asks. "Movie night?"

"You've got popcorn, right?" Charlie doesn't even wait for him to give permission. Of course they can have the living room. They can have the whole house.

Raya's halfway to the kitchen, making for the cupboard. "Let's see!"

"What's that smell?" Bells lifts her head like a dog. "Are you cooking, Dad?"

Absolutely, I'm cooking! *I've got to fucking poison your friends somehow.* "Pot roast."

"Gravy? Rolls?" Bells loves rolls.

"You betcha. Be ready in about an hour."

Raya pulls a jar of popcorn kernels out of the cupboard. "Jackpot!"

"Perfect," Charlie chants. "Let's go do that stupid English homework, then we'll be ready for dinner. What movie are we going to watch?"

"We'll fight over it," Bells reasons. "After that absurd essay. Let's at least do an outline."

They go off to Bells' room. Threader sits down at the table as the door closes and takes a deep breath. He looks at his hand. It's shaking. His heart is moving quick, too. *Goddammit.* He doesn't want to kill the girls. For the first time since he took over for his father, he realizes he doesn't want to follow the demon's rules.

But he has to. That's the simple truth. Want to or not. If they make a request, he does it. Look at everything they've given him in return. A nice house. Money in the bank account. Good cars. A way to take care of his kid. All thanks to the demon's influence. Things just work out for him. He never has to try too hard. And he's strong. He's fast. He's fit as a fiddle. Doesn't have to work out, either. It's them. They take care of him.

His family has been doing this job for as long as anyone seems to know. Long before World War 1, long before the Civil War, even. One male heir after another inheriting the right of power. 'Least until Threader bites it or gets caught, then Bells will come, and she'll be the first girl as far as he knows. He doesn't think she'll have it in her, but that's not really for him to decide. Imagining her doing the bidding of the demons makes him feel a bit funny. Could she kill someone? Could she kill someone she knew and loved? He doubts it. Bells is sweeter than a dandelion.

But he can kill. He can get his hands wet with blood. His Dad never kept that much from him. He was helping before he was 11 or 12, digging holes and playing helpless to distract people, once or twice he even lured people to their doom. It all made sense to him. Dad needed some help occasionally. Dad was in his 40's when Threader was born, and that old truck driver's back didn't make things easy on him. The demons kept him spry as they could, he guessed, but what are you going to do?

The back is what eventually got him caught. He twisted it on the job, twisted it so bad he could barely get back up and move. He was caught red handed, and once he was caught, they started tying a lot of shit back to him. Looking at his trucking path they found a damn long list of missing persons. It was circumstantial, but it was enough, combined with the fresh blood on his hands, to lock him up for good.

Threader's got a good back, though, and he hasn't been so clumsy. He learned from that. The demons learned a little, too. Maybe if he does end up going away, they'll be easier on Bells. Or maybe they'll just move on to some other family with men to do the dirty work. Who knows? He hopes that's what it is.

He sits at the table and listens to the girl's chattering through Bells closed door. A few minutes before the timer is set to go off, he takes the pot roast out of the oven. Carrots, potatoes, gravy, rolls. It's not a half bad last meal. The medicine is ground up in a tiny tin in his pocket. He takes it out, collects four bowls, and carefully measures a pinch into three healthy servings. He sets the table: placemats, spoons, forks, rolls, finally the bowls of stew. He leaves cups with ice on the counter.

"Girls!" Dad calls from the kitchen. "You've gotta be finished with a damn outline by now. Let's eat."

They look between each other grimly. Raya seems like she's finally feeling a touch of fear. Charlie is still calm. Bells is feeling sick. Suddenly, she doesn't want to do this. He's so oblivious—so harmless, at least to them—it feels wrong. It feels totally wrong.

"Don't quit on us now," Charlie hisses.

Bells mutters a weak defense. "I'm not."

"Can see it on your face," Raya insists. "You're having second thoughts."

"It's just—" she lowers her voice, glancing at the door "—it's just, *do we really even need to do this*?"

"I knew it," Charlie growls. "I freaking knew it."

"We could just ask him," Bells whispers. "We could literally just ask. Tell him we know and see what he says."

"And then lose our chance to ever take it?" Raya asks.

"*He's going to give it to me eventually, isn't he*?" The responsibility and power has been in her family for generations. Passed down from father to son—but what will they do when there's no son? Surely she'll get it. Surely.

"We could have anything we wanted," Charlie reminds her. "Anything at all, Bells. Money. Cars. Power. College. They're *powerful*. If we test it, I bet we can figure out how to get way more than your dad is getting. If they really trust us and need us."

Bells stands up abruptly and goes to the door. Charlie's fiddling with a 4 inch knife in her pocket. Raya has one, too, but it's hidden somewhere. She isn't messing with it. Bells' knife is in her drawer. She thinks about going to get it and then shakes her head. No. She's not going to deliver the fatal blow. That much she simply can't do.

"Fine," she concedes. "Let's go. I bet neither of you have the guts to do it, anyway. But if you do, fine. I won't stop you."

She steps into the hall alone and the girls hasten to keep up. Dad's got the table set. He's already sitting down and buttering his roll. He has a book out, something that looks like science fiction. Would he be upset if he knew he was never going to get to finish it?

She looks over her shoulder. Raya and Charlie have twin expressions of determination. Maybe they really will do it. Who the heck knows?

Bells sits across from her dad. Raya and Charlie sit across from each other. In that way, they're both next to him. Either of them could strike out. Would he be quick enough to stop one of them? Probably. But both at the same time? It seems unlikely.

Her heart is beating like mad. She takes a quick bite of stew to try and cover up how freaked out she is. Charlie and Raya pick up their spoons, too, and that calms her down a little. Dad's got his mouth stuffed, he always pigs out. He's a sitting duck.

She starts to wolf down the stew because she's so nervous. Charlie shoots her an annoyed glance. She's eating slow. Raya has only had a few bites.

Dad looks up from his bowl for the first time. "What's your essay a —"

That's when Charlie strikes. She had the knife out under the table the whole time. She brings it into sight and strikes quicker than Bells would have thought possible. It's a flash, and she's been expecting it.

But Dad's fast. She knew he was fast. Amazingly, he reacts. It looks like she was aiming for his neck, but he flinches in time to deflect the blow slightly. The knife hits him under the arm, popping into his chest like a shot at the doctor's office.

He lets out a gasp. Charlie's on her feet. She starts to pull it out and stumbles, almost like she's been hit herself.

"Wha—?"

"Goddammit!" Dad roars. He's clutching his chest and he pushes his chair back. His face is pained and confused. "God Jesus dammit, what in the hell is wrong with you?" He looks at Bells, then at Raya. "What in the—"

Raya's on her feet. She has her knife out. She goes for him, charging a bit like a drunk, and Dad holds out a hand to drive her off. She slashes at his arm and the knife connects, making a deep cut. But she's too close. He grabs her, pulls her into a kind of hug, and crushes her into his chest. He squeezes tight, tighter, like a freak human-anaconda hybrid, until Raya drops her knife and screams for help.

"Help!" she wheezes. "Bells, please! He..." he tightens his grip. She kicks her legs, flails her arms. He squeezes even tighter, until his eyes are bulging, until *her* eyes are bulging. Then she goes limp and he drops her.

Bells tries to stand, but realizes she can't with a bit of panic. What in the hell is going on? Are her nerves really this bad? She looks at Charlie and can't make sense of what's happening. Something is wrong with her, too. Dad's bleeding steadily on his arm and the wound in his side is pumping blood. Charlie must have hit something major.

"What in the hell have you done this for?" He looks at Charlie, sees he won't get an answer, and then turns to Bells.

She's still sitting in the same spot as when it all began. Her legs don't work. Her vision is blurry. Is she having some kind of panic attack? She can't think straight, or see much at all. She's so light-headed she can barely think.

"I think I'm going to be sick," the voice that comes from her throat is slurred and weak.

Dad starts to come for her. Charlie reaches out for him, stabbing with the knife, and lands on the upper part of his thigh. He screams mightily and backhands her with enough strength to send her reeling. She flies into the wall, shaking the whole house. Every picture in the kitchen falls onto the tile.

Dad spins. The knife is still in his leg. He pulls it out, screaming, and dives for Charlie.

The last thing Bells sees is him bringing the knife down into Charlie's skull. Once, twice, he lifts it again, blood sprays, and then she loses sight of it all.

This isn't how it was supposed to happen, she thinks. *I didn't want it to be like this. Inheritances aren't supposed to be this messy.*

Don't Cross *by Anna Vaks*

A
Portland
Nightmare

The man had been following her for a few streets. Jenny had a good sense for guys like him. She could almost tell just from looking at a man if he was good or bad. The moment this guy fell in behind her and started following—she took two lefts and then a right down Waterfront, not a reasonable path for anyone to actually be taking—she got bumps all up and down her arms.

He was following her. At fifteen, and homeless for nearly two years, she knew all about what guys would do to you if you let them follow you and got caught in a lonely place. She had a knife in her pocket, but he was big enough that if they got close, there was a good chance he'd knock it out of her hand before she could really stick him with it. In Portland, she figured there was a good chance that would happen to her, if for no other reason than the news needed something sad to talk about in the morning. 'Course it was pretty optimistic of her to think anyone would care about a little homeless girl being raped and killed.

She was heading for the park. It wasn't quite sundown, and lots of times people were still in the park around this time of day. She figured the chances were 50-50 that she was about to fight, but the thought of that had her heart running fast. Adrenaline was starting to pump swiftly through her veins, and her pulse was river-quick.

Jenny sped up when she heard footsteps behind her. There'd been a careful pretense up to that moment, one which said—*I don't know you're following me, and so you don't need to chase me yet.* But he'd been speeding up without her noticing, and he'd closed the distance behind them by about half. That wasn't good. She only became aware of that fact in the moment that she heard the approaching steps. The man's steps were heavy, which meant he was heavy, which meant if he fell on her, she'd never be able to get him off.

Headlights blinked over a hilltop and a yellow taxi came zipping down the road merrily. She felt a wave of hope and tried to flag it down. She had no money, and didn't have a destination, but the driver couldn't know that just by seeing her.

The car slowed slightly. The noise of the engine cut out as the driver let off the gas. She could see him in the car, pausing to take her in, considering...

She waved her hands frantically and started to step into the street. *Let him run me over*, she thought grimly. *I'd rather be roadkill than thrown in the ditch after this guy behind me does whatever it is he's wanting to do.*

The driver gritted his teeth when she stepped into the road and swerved around her, hitting the gas hard. Jenny lunged for the car, as if she might be able to grab it in the way she used to grab her older sisters shirt in a game of tag. She was late, though, and slow. The back of her hand barely grazed the trunk.

She'd spun full around in her desperation.

Suddenly, she was face to face with the creep. He'd paused about twenty feet away, still on the sidewalk. He had an overgrown mustache, a sunburned, chubby face, and his clothes were too clean for him to be homeless.

She scanned the street quickly. Her heart welled into her throat as her eyes saw what her mind and sixth sense had already known. They were alone. The taxi driver sped away, red taillights fading into the dusk.

The man smiled at her. His mustache lifted with his lip, revealing a mouthful of stained and crooked teeth.

Jenny turned and ran.

Her shoes were old enough that they were starting to come apart, and as she took off and got up to full speed, the heel on her left foot gave way. She stumbled, almost careened into a bush, and only managed to keep upright from luck.

At her back, steadily gaining, she could hear the pounding feet and heavy breaths of the gap toothed man. She was fast—had won the blue ribbon in track and field three grades in a row—but he was getting closer anyway.

She looked over her shoulder to confirm. He was just behind her now, a few lengths away. Any second he'd be able to stretch out his arm and grab the back of her thin coat. If she were lucky, the tattered fabric would rip and he'd stumble and she'd somehow keep on her feet. But she was never lucky these days.

Her feet were numb from pounding the street. Her eyes were starting to water from stress, and her breath was coming harder. She tried to pull in a big lungful of air, but a sharp pain is all she got. She heaved another, quicker, and suddenly she was gasping.

She veered hard off the sidewalk and onto a little path full of shrubs and tall elms that led into the park. That's when she felt the tug on the back of her jacket, and screamed. There was hot breath on the back of her neck, and an awful, grating grunt in her ear.

She grabbed for the knife in her pocket, pulled it free, turned rapidly, and slashed.

She caught the man in the face. She'd misjudged his height—remembering him taller than he really was—and missed his throat. Still, that got his hands to go limp. She brought her free hand down hard, pushing him away and knocking his outstretched arms aside.

He howled wordlessly and brought his hands up to his face. A great well of blood was spilling and spewing from the gash, which ran from the bottom of his chin to just beneath his right eye.

Jenny started to run again, and nearly crashed into the kids.

A set of hands shot out to catch her before she fell back toward the man. They were friendly hands, she could tell at once, and the face that belonged to them didn't want to hurt her.

She blinked, nonplussed, and took in the unexpected but welcome group as the man continued screaming just a few feet behind them.

There was a tall girl in the back of the group of kids. Three boys stood in front of her. Jenny figured they were all around the same age, somewhere in high school—assuming they were still in school. None of them looked like they had clean clothes or showers, and their bags were stuffed full of things that weren't books.

The girl asked, "What in the hell did you get him like that for?"

"He was chasing me," Jenny said, sidling back to put more space between herself and the would-be attacker. "I tried to run but he caught me."

The boy who'd caught her—the biggest and oldest looking one of the bunch—stepped forward and punched the guy without further explanation. The blow caught the man right in the jaw, and he went sprawling back like a court jester who'd lost his balance.

He landed hard on the pavement and didn't move.

The boy turned back around with a surprised expression on his face. Like he couldn't quite believe what he'd done. "I got him!"

"Bastard deserved it," the girl said simply, shrugging. Then she turned to Jenny and held out her hand. "Hi. I'm Sam."

Jenny shook her hand. The action felt adult-like and weird, considering none of them looked old enough to even buy a pack of cigarettes. They were kids, just like her. Probably homeless, or at least in halfway homes. Sam had a big splash of freckles on her nose, and a birthmark on her cheek. Jenny thought it made her look mysterious.

"I'm Bradley," the tall boy said. He stuck his hand out—the same one he punched the attacker with—and Jenny shook it gladly.

Bradley thumbed over his back at the remaining two boys. "That's Jerry and Jude. They're brothers. Folks kicked them out a year ago, they've been running with Sam and me ever since."

Jenny waved at the brothers, who looked exactly alike except that one was pretty chubby and the other was thin as a rail. She wasn't positive which was which, and didn't want to ask. Her heart was only just calming down. She was sweaty and still a little scared.

"I thought he was going to get me," she finally said.

The four of them laughed, all at the same time, like she'd told a joke.

"I'm serious!"

Sam smiled at her. "It kind of seems like you had him handled."

Bradley motioned to her hand, which she only then remembered was still clutched tightly around her bloody knife. "You gonna use that on one of us?"

She shoved it into her pocket nervously. "'Course not! I'm not a freak. The guy was *attacking* me. Didn't you hear me yelling?"

"Matter of fact," the fat brother said with a country drawl, "we heard ya huffin and puffin 'cause we was on the other side of that there wall of June bushes."

"Quiet, Jude," the skinny brother, who Jenny now knew was called Jerry, growled. "She wasn't huffin and puffin no more than you would if I gave chase to ya, huh?"

Jude blinked at his brother thoughtfully, then shrugged. "I guess not."

The guy on the ground moaned, then, and Jenny skipped a few feet away from him. "Ugh," she said. "He gives me the absolute creeps. What do you think he would have done to me if I didn't have this knife?"

"Raped you," Jude said instantly.

"Killed you," Jerry agreed.

"Beat you really bad, chew you up, spit you out." Bradley nodded. "Yep. We know his type."

Sam said nothing at all. She only glared at the man as he stirred slightly on the ground. He was lying in a pool of sticky blood. It was still dripping freely from the cut on his face.

"Should end him right there," she said darkly.

Jenny gaped at her. "You mean *kill* him?"

Sam looked deadly serious. "He deserves it."

The brothers looked at one another with raised brows. Then they looked at Bradley. Jenny looked at Bradley, too, cause he seemed the oldest and like the one in charge. He put a hand on Sam's shoulder.

"We should just leave him there. He might have learned his lesson."

"Might not have," Sam said darkly. "What if Jenny hadn't had a knife? What if we hadn't heard her? The next girl might not be so lucky."

"We're not going to kill him," Bradley said flatly. "Let's get out of here."

Sam looked like she wanted to argue, but Jude and Jerry turned and started walking away. They seemed to pull her along without really meaning to. Her feet just started following them, like she was in their orbit somehow. The same thing happened to Bradley as Sam started moving. He moved like he was pulled along by her.

Jenny watched, thoughtful, and felt a little pang realizing that she'd never felt something like that before. No one had ever pulled her along, no one had ever made her feel like she *could* be pulled along.

Bradley turned, still walking, and waved at her. "Well, are you coming or what?"

The gap-toothed man stirred again, groaning, and that made up her mind for her.

"Yeah."

Jude and Jerry kept up a steady stream of commentary while the five of them walked through town. It was full dark out, now, and getting cold, but all of them were used to the cold and so didn't mind it too much. Bradley was walking right alongside her, and Jenny wondered if people who saw them would think they were a couple. She looked up at him and hoped they would.

They paused at a street corner to wait for traffic. The stream of traffic was steady now, they weren't so far from the bridge. Jenny knew this place, there was a shelter a street or so down, and a good Chinese food place that would sell you a whole carton of fried rice for $2. Sometimes it even had gristly chicken in it.

Jude was pontificating on the advantages and disadvantages of being fat and homeless when the light turned red, and the crosswalk symbol lit up. Jenny was lost in thought, wondering where the group was going, and stepped out into the street from reflex.

"Wait!"

She turned toward the sudden blare of a panicked horn, HONNKKK, heart flying into her throat, and had a single second to realize how stupid she was before the car was on her. She could feel the bumper, she could see the driver's shocked and furious face, she could hear the engine rumbling beneath the hood, waiting to drive right over her without even missing a beat. She imagined what the tires would feel like, flattening her bones and squeezing her guts out like jelly from a doughnut.

Someone grabbed her by the waist, and in the moment the car was going to flatten her, she was pulled back. The breath went *whoosh* out of her chest, her neck snapped from the abrupt force of being yanked and grabbed. She lost her balance and started to fall—whoever was behind her fell with her. They sprawled out on the sidewalk, coming down hard, but she didn't even feel it.

"Holy crap!" someone—she thought Jude—exploded.

Sam sounded more concerned and less excited. "Is she all right? Give her some air!"

Jenny blinked and the world came back into place. Her heart finally realized what'd happened and started to beat rapidly again. Her stupid, overused adrenal gland came back to life, too, and for the second time in half an hour it flooded her with chemicals that made her eyes jitter and jump.

She rolled over and saw Bradley sprawled out beside her. His eyes were round as manhole grates, and he was grinning hugely.

"Holy smokes," he laughed. "You never learn to look both ways before you cross the street?"

She shook her head meekly. "I wasn't thinking."

Sam stood over her and reached out a hand to help her up. "You got that right. That was some *Final Destination shit*. Maybe that guy was supposed to get you after all."

Jenny laughed at that. Bradley did, too.

They stood up and dusted themselves off. The commotion caught the attention of some passersby on the other end of the street. People were looking at them and pointing. Someone had their phone out and was recording.

"What the heck are they recording us for?" Jerry complained. "Never seen a gang of homeless kids nearly get run over by a car?"

Jenny rolled her eyes. By then, the crosswalk had turned again and the lights were green. Engines revved and the steady stream of traffic took the street back over. That was just as well, she still needed a minute to compose herself. It's not every day you nearly get killed twice in half an hour.

"So where are we going, anyway?" she ventured.

The four of them looked between each other.

Bradley broke the quiet. "Where do you normally spend the night? We got a place that's pretty safe."

She shrugged evasively. It wasn't cool to ask homeless people where they spent the night, normally, cause that was pretty private. "Depends on my fancy. Normally nowhere good."

Sam nodded knowingly. "It's hard when you're alone. Do you have any people?"

"No," Jenny said simply. "Not for a while at least. I knew this woman, but I guess she left town or something."

"Happened to me once with an old guy," Bradley said. "We were tight for a few weeks. Next thing I know he's gone. Sucked."

"That's why I like you guys," Sam said. "All of you stink too bad to ever leave."

"I resent that," Jude declared solemnly. "All manner of people are willing to tolerate my stink."

"Your own momma wasn't willing," Jerry snapped.

Jude blinked at him, seeming to try and decide if he was offended by that or not. When Sam and Bradley started laughing, he figured it was funny and joined them. Jenny laughed too. It felt good to laugh— and weird. Is this how you made friends? She hadn't had one since middle school, years and years ago, and frankly wasn't sure anymore.

"You can come with us if you want," Sam said, directly extending the invitation for the first time. "It's hard out here when you're alone. We need to stick together with good people if we can."

"I got a $20 from some guy in a suit this morning," Jerry said. "Was planning on pizza. You like pepperoni?"

All she'd had since that morning was a doughnut. She admitted as much, and Sam put her arm around her shoulder and pulled her into a hug. "You're coming with us, or *else*. Eat until you can't move, and if you want to leave after, that's fine. But at least eat."

This time when the light turned red and the crosswalk lit up, Jenny looked both ways. Bradley made a show about stopping traffic and waving them all across, like he was a safety police. Jerry and Jude spun all about, looking every which way, as if they were playing a game of dodge ball.

It took around fifteen minutes to get to their spot. It was an old convenience store across the street from a major grocery chain. It was dark and boarded up, definitely off limits, but no one much checked these places anyway.

"It's not a castle or nothin'," Jude warbled, pretending to be embarrassed. "But it's home!"

Sam scoffed at him. "Lay off, dork."

Bradley led the way. They circled around to the back of the building, where one of the boarded windows had been removed. Jenny tried to see inside, but it was too dark. Bradley may as well have climbed into a cave. Jerry followed him, and there was some weird scuffling sounds before a light suddenly flared to life.

It was an old candle. She could see Bradley and Jerry clearly, then, and the room they were in. It was shockingly clean. There were a few beds inside, some clothes and blankets, a table—even an old bookcase with some magazines and novels on the shelves.

"Holy crap," Jenny gasped. "You guys have a whole *house* in here."

Sam beamed at her. "You can stay as long as you want. Really. I need another girl here to help me fend off these gross guys."

More candles were lit, and by the time Jenny climbed inside, it was well lit enough to study the dirt under your fingernails or read one of the books that sat on the dilapidated bookshelf they no doubt found near a dumpster.

Sam showed her around. There were five mattresses, a few nightstands, candles scattered everywhere, several old magazines lying about (one of which was for adults), and some curious looking books. A few suitcases, littered with clothes and random belongings, evidenced that they'd been here for quite some time.

The more she looked, the more surprised she was at how clean it was. There was no trash or dirt. If it had power, Jenny would think they owned the place and belonged there.

"This place is amazing," she finally said.

The four of them smiled at her happily. "We've been fixing it up for a few months."

She nodded at the fifth mattress, which didn't appear to get used often. "Why do you have five beds, though?"

A look passed between Bradley and Sam. It was a brief glance, one they perhaps didn't mean for her to see, but she noticed it all the same.

Jude answered when neither of them did. "We always wanna be able to help, you know?"

Jenny tried not to act suspicious or weird. They were being nice to her—they'd saved her life twice in half an hour—the last thing they deserved was for her to be paranoid or suspicious. But being homeless, that was about all she could be. Nothing good had happened to her in years. It seemed impossible to let her guard down.

"No one ever slept on it," Jerry said. "'Least not since we stole it from some tent a bunch of city kids set up in their backyard out over in the ritzy neighborhood thataway—" he pointed toward the city's outskirts.

"Jeez, don't tell her we're thieves," Sam hissed.

Jenny giggled at that. "Did you really think I'd figure you bought all this stuff at the discount store?"

Bradley held the back of his head self-consciously. "Guess not. You don't think we're so bad though, huh? We've got to get by somehow, right?"

She nodded seriously. "I don't think you're so bad." Then she repeated her earlier assessment. "This place is amazing."

And it was. A few minutes later, Jerry and Jude volunteered to go get the pizzas, Sam insisted on showing Jenny around the neighborhood and going on a soda run, and Bradley decided to go with them. She was already familiar with the place, but acted politely interested as they showed her around. She figured she knew just about everywhere in Portland by now, especially the Steel Bridge and the areas around it.

Used to, when she was first homeless, Jenny would stand at the edge of the bridge and contemplate diving into the Willamette. It's not so big a fall as to kill someone, but she can't swim, and the water's so cold in winter, she figured it'd kill you fast from shock. Something always held her back though.

They crossed over it, Sam talking all the while about the quirks of their neighborhood and the people you had to look out for versus the people who were pretty decent. She talked like Jenny had already promised she'd stay forever. She talked like they'd been friends for years. Bradley just walked on, nodding and smiling from time to time.

Later, after they got the sodas and got back to the abandoned convenience store, after pizza had been doled out and eaten and everyone was stretched out and gasping from how much food they'd eaten, Jenny got to looking around a little more.

Jude and Jerry passed out within half an hour. Sam took to reading an old magazine, and Bradley was studying a book intently. She tried to see what the title was, but all she could make out was a curious diagram on the front of it. It looked a bit like the Star of David, only the lines were a little off, and it had a circle around it.

She wanted to ask him about it, but he was across the room and she figured waking up Jerry and Jude would be rude, so she laid back instead. She thought about her old pad—a decent blanket with some cardboard, pulled up beneath a bridge where a few other homeless people slept—and didn't miss it one bit. This was nicer than a shelter by far, just about the nicest place she'd stayed since she had to leave home.

To her surprise, she felt sleepy after no time at all. Even after all the days excitement, even being some place unfamiliar, with unfamiliar people, she managed to drift off within a few minutes. She slept all night, without dreaming much at all, and only woke up because the sunrise came right in through the window and fell onto her sleeping face.

The others were still asleep. She needed to use the bathroom, so she went through the window and did her business behind a bush. There were a few people walking the street, and a few cars, but she was out of sight.

When she climbed back in, she noticed the book again, lying just beside Bradley's mattress. She peered around the room surreptitiously, confirming no one was awake. Jerry and Jude slept on their backs, with their hands folded neatly over their chests like vampires. Weird. Sam slept on her stomach with her head shoved into a pillow, like she was trying to suffocate herself. Bradley slept on his side, facing her, with his eyes gently closed.

She crept next to him and reached for the book. She watched his face all the while for any sign that he was waking up. Her lips were slightly parted, and his breathing was shallow and calm. He was surely asleep, fast asleep. He wouldn't know she was snooping.

She laid her hand on the bare leather-bound cover, touching the encircled Star of David, and finally could read the title: THE BOOK OF THE DEAD: COMMUNING WITH THE OCCULT. The realization that it wasn't a Star of David at all, but a pentagram, and that the book was concerned with some kind of devil worship, sent a horrible chill through her body.

Still, she picked up the book and held it carefully in her hands. The cover was heavy, and felt good under her hands. She flipped it open, thumbing through the opening pages to get to the glossary. *Like a freaking textbook*, she thought sarcastically, half amazed and half scared.

There was a bookmark stuck roughly halfway into the book. She went to it, then, and squinted hard to read the title of the chapter in the low light. SACRIFICE: The Final Step. Her breath was shallow just from reading that, and her heart was beginning to pick up the pace. She waited for the touch of adrenaline and was relieved when it didn't come. The adrenaline made her vision tighter and blurry at the same time, and it made her legs feel jittery. The adrenaline warned her that she was in for it—and the fact that it wasn't there made her feel safe, somehow.

She started reading as quick as she could, still frozen to the spot. The book detailed various things which must be true about the sacrifice. They needed to be young, a virgin, a girl, and die in exquisite pain. The body must be burned while alive, and while dead, and a certain number of cuts and a certain amount of blood must be extolled before the sacrifice was allowed to die.

In short, the chapter went into express and careful detail about how, exactly, to torture and kill a person in order to sacrifice them to *The Power*. The Power, whatever it was, must have been explained in the earlier chapters. There was no attempt to express what The Power might do for you, or what you might actually gain—only the steps involved to perform the sacrifice.

She'd read all she needed to read. Maybe more than was wise, considering she knew the moment she read the title that something was up.

The fifth mattress and the look between Sam and Bradley came back to mind now, and she realized, horribly and frightfully, what that might mean. Had they lured someone else here and killed them, before? Did the book say they needed to do it again, or had it perhaps not gone exactly to plan? Did they botch the murder, and have to do a repeat?

There was too much to consider, but the threat was real and starting to press on her chest in a way that made it hard to take a full breath. She had to get the hell out of there, and fast.

She turned for the window, still holding onto the book out of fear— and yelped when she came face to face with Sam. Impossibly, the tall girl had woken up and got out of bed without making a sound. Or maybe the pounding blood rushing through her ears made her oblivious. Nonetheless, she was there, now, standing face to face with her, smiling slightly and shaking her head back and forth, just like Jenny's mom used to do when she caught her pulling the peanut butter out of the pantry.

"I—"

"You read something that doesn't belong to you," Sam interrupted harshly. Her face was sterner and meaner than it had been all of yesterday, except in the moment she suggested they kill the man who'd been chasing Jenny.

"Bradley," she snapped. "Wake the hell up. Jerry, Jude!"

Jenny felt her chances of escaping rapidly dwindling, and did the only thing she could think to do. She reached into her pocket for her knife and made to stab at Sam's belly. If she could only knock her down and make the window, she could run into the street and scream for help.

But Sam saw the move coming like she'd known it was what she was going to try and do. She grabbed Jenny's arm before she could even turn the knife fully around, and her grip was like iron. She felt supernaturally strong, and the moment her grip tightened on her forearms and her jaw clenched and her face transformed a little into a kind of grin, Jenny knew she was caught and done for.

Sam drove her back into the wall and Jenny half stumbled, half fell across the room. She hit the wall hard and banged her head good enough to blur her vision for a moment.

"Jeez!" she cried numbly. "Get the hell—"

To her surprise, Sam did release her grip, fast—but just as quick she'd whipped her hand around and slapped her in the face so hard her head spun around. Her neck twisted from the hard hit, and the taste of blood instantly filled her mouth.

"Gah!"

When she blinked the world back into place, she saw the boys were up. Bradley had a long knife in his hands, and Jerry and Jude each had grabbed belts that must have been hidden somewhere in their luggage.

"We're gonna tie you up," Sam said, breathing heavily as if she was the one who'd just been slapped so hard she saw stars, and not the other way around. "And—"

Jenny screamed then, sucking a huge torrent of air into her chest and then hollering with all her might. "*Hellllppppp!*" She sucked in another breath, preparing to scream again, and Sam knocked the wind right out of her lungs with a punch to the belly that doubled her over and made her wheeze like an old man with smokers cough.

"Tie her up," Sam shouted furiously. "Tie her the fuck up and get ready to do this thing *right* this time."

The brother's moved forward with their belts. Sam stepped aside.

"Don't forget the book," Sam griped at Bradley. "We can't afford to mess this up again. We have to do it right."

"We will," Bradley said flatly. He'd picked the book up from where

Jenny dropped it, and he was holding it like a baby. "We will."

Final Stop *by Roval Tarroza*

SUICIDE BRIDGE

He was up against a deadline and thought, probably, this would be the last straw if he didn't make it. His editor's back wouldn't break like a camel, but he'd get fired just the same, and that was good enough to light a hot fire under Jerry's ass. Journalism wasn't what it once was, what with the $100 breakfasts and the free hotel rooms and the $10,000 yearly bonuses. No, these days you were lucky just to have a job. And if you didn't do it well, hell, they'd drop you like a hot cake.

The Portland Eye, the joint he'd been working for since the century turned over, churned and burned through four separate writers this year alone, and a pair of editors. The one they had now, a severe woman that used to work for CNN, made Jerry feel rightly threatened for his job.

He was half asleep on the MAX Light Rail, pondering what he'd done in the last life to deserve this. A bum tip led him all the way out to Beaverton, and after wasting away half the afternoon slogging it on the pavement, he'd finally given up and decided to head home. This was supposed to be his big break. Instead, all it got him was a goddamned splitting headache and a sore big toe. His shoes were starting to come apart. He needed a new pair, but Mary would have his ass if he went out and spent $80 on a pair of shoes when he told her they couldn't afford the name brand formula for the new baby just a few weeks ago.

And it was true. They couldn't afford the name brand formula.

They could barely afford to keep the lights on. He didn't tell his wife anything about the trouble at work, and she was so consumed with the kids that he thought she didn't have a damn idea how stressed he was. Which was a shame, because even the hollow-eyed stares of the homeless he passed by on the streets seemed to recognize just how fucked he was feeling lately. 'Course, Mary would have had to look at him to see how big the bags were under his eyes and see the stress lines, which he was positive weren't there earlier this year, forming up so heavily at the creases of his eyes and in the middle of his forehead. Lately, it seemed like she purposefully found something else to look at when he walked into the room.

The guy he was supposed to meet hadn't shown. He'd contacted him by phone a few days ago, sounding harried and stressed, and asked, "Is this Jerry Buchemei?"

Jerry had felt, for no particular reason, that the call was important. "It is."

"Hey man—" a pause so long Jerry took the phone from his ear to check that the call hadn't disconnected "—you're doing a story on the factory?"

That got his attention all right, and for a moment, he was speechless. "Not exactly."

"Well do you want to know what I know, or not? I don't have much proof, but I guess you're used to that."

Jerry told him that he did, indeed, want to know what he knew. The factory in question—one he wouldn't name, even in his own mind—was more secretive and guarded than the fucking Pentagon. He'd been working on a piece about it, trying to pull at the loose threads that poked out of the tightly lidded box that made it up, since he first began investigative journalism, nearly 20 years ago. Like had happened many times in his career, the factory was rearing its ugly head again as he was trying to work on an unrelated story, now.

They made plans to meet. The fellow told him he'd be in a red suit. Ostentatious, Jerry thought—but at least he'd know him when he saw him. Of course when the time came, the damn guy was nowhere to be found. Jerry was used to it, but even so, it hurt. He let himself hope every time. That was his mistake. He kept thinking it'd be different.

He gazed out of the dirty window and sighed heavily. Portland wasn't what it once was. Things seemed to be degrading, not just in his life. If the drug epidemic hadn't doubled the amount of homeless and at-risk in the last decade, he'd eat his torn-up shoes. The piece he was currently working on was about violence among youth in the foster care system, and by extension violent crime among young adults across the whole city, seemed to keep circling back around to that trouble. Drugs, poverty, homelessness—and of course the factory.

Jerry thought, sometimes, that everything had somehow gone wrong. When he was a kid, a man working full time could keep the family afloat; two cars, a house, a good line of credit at the store, all the new toys. These days, the same god damn job that ran 50 years ago at the auto plant was making less money, and things were well over double the cost. It didn't make sense. It didn't make a lick of sense to him. The city was falling down around them. Quality of life was decreasing. The air quality was going to shit. Debt per person had skyrocketed, and wages were stagnant not for a decade, not for two decades, but damn near 30 years straight.

But you'd better believe the rich were a hell of a lot richer. The old couple who owned The Portland Eye, you'd better fucking believe they'd bought a third house and a nice "Light Yacht" – which was rich person code for "A yacht that only costs a few million dollars, because we're well off, but not rich enough to have schemed up a way to profit off the child slaves in Taiwan and China yet." No, they were just profiting off drowning middle (now edging well under the middle) class folks like him. Jerry felt like a damn clown at the stupid Christmas parties, smiling and nodding, kissing ass, and for what? It's not like they'd given him a cost-of-living raise. It's not like he got a bonus. No, no, things at The Portland Eye were slim, if you asked HR, no one could get approved for a raise this year, no matter how well they'd performed. But he happened to know his new editor had been cajoled into quitting her position at CNN with a fancy sign on bonus from the CEO.

It's not like there was less money in the world, or less money in

Portland. That's the thing that really got him going. There were plenty of hard working men and women slogging away day after day, plenty of business. The money was just being funneled, more and more, year after year, to the bastards that owned yachts and less and less to the poor saps actually out doing the work.

It was enough to make Jerry want to scream. The title of his piece was: CRIME ON THE RISE—ARE THE YOUTH TO BLAME? You'd better believe he didn't come up with that, because it was a mockery of the real story, the one he'd been uncovering for weeks—and now, with the threat of a guillotine hanging over his head, he felt like there wasn't a thing to do but write the shit article he'd been tasked with writing, even knowing it was, ethically, the wrong thing to do.

The youth weren't to blame for violence in Portland, no more than the youth were to blame for homelessness and drug addiction. The government was to blame, and the ultra-rich snobs who lobbied the government into allowing them to steal more and more of the profits they made right off the backs of their fellow American's year after year.

He spent weeks trying to find the right angle. Jerry could be convincing when he needed to be. He pushed his deadline back more than once, he made excuses, he fought to get the story right. Portland needed the story right, he said. And he meant that.

But every time he got a lead—a well-known businessman that ran the second largest company in the city who was smuggling profits out from beneath his investors (and out from beneath his employees)—or the chemical factory on the Willamette that was skirting regulations and avoiding inspections, who hadn't gotten proper permits in several decades—something seemed to conspire against him.

He could still hear the guy's voice. Paranoid, maybe edging on schizoid. But there was a note of truth there. Jerry had been at the job long enough that he couldn't be fooled easily. The guy was the real deal. He'd had something.

So why hadn't he shown?

It was his last chance, and he'd come up double zero. He just couldn't get his fingers under the lid of the coffin hiding all this dreadful shit. He needed more time. A few years ago, maybe he would have rolled the dice. But now he had Denny and Beth to think about. Mary would hate him forever if he lost his job because he was trying to stand on a moral high ground. He'd deserve to be hated forever.

A man had to care for his family before he could care for his city. For Jerry, that meant swallowing his pride. That was hard to accept, though, as the MAX continued zipping him along the clammy city streets. He took his eyes away from the sorry sights and turned them inward. The inside of the train was cleaner than half the restaurants he'd been in this month. The city could take care of the MAX, but they couldn't take care of the streets.

A pair of teenagers were leaning back at the front of his car. An older, grizzled looking black man sat across from them. He was reading a newspaper, glasses on the tip of his nose, cap pulled down nearly over his eyes. The teenagers were both scrolling through their phones.

Jerry turned and looked in the back of the car. There was an older woman in a maid's uniform, looking thoroughly worn out, and a schoolgirl with her mother. The girl looked sick, and the mother looked annoyed. Outside, the city continued flying by. Someone slammed on their brakes and the sound of tires skidding almost made him turn his head, but he resisted the urge, studying the people around him instead. A few horns blared a moment later. Still, he didn't look outside.

They were approaching Jefferson Street, moving downtown. He only had a few more minutes to rest his aching feet. His big toe was really hurting. He thought he'd look for a pair of lightly used shoes at the thrift store tomorrow, as a reward for writing the article he truly didn't want to write.

All his research had led him nowhere. That simple fact hurt, cause he'd put so much more time into this than he was supposed to. He was going to end up with a heartless and bland retelling of the statistics and the troubling stories he'd initially found in the first two days of research, with no way to explain his weeks of dragging feet.

The theory he'd been working on was like this: crime in Portland was on the rise because poverty was on the rise. Drugs and poverty went hand in hand. In the midst of this awful cycle of poverty and drugs begetting violence and crime, there were a select few among them —truly a select few—who were growing richer, and happier, and safer. And they were doing so at the cost of nearly every man, woman, and child in the city of Portland.

It was a bigger story than that, on the macro level, of course. Not just a Portland thing, not just an Oregon thing, not even just an America thing. It was like this in nearly every country in the world. The rich had figured out a way to game the system, and it was on the heads and backs of the poor fellows like him and that maid in the back of the bus and the old man reading the paper in the front. The teenagers scrolling on their phone—what did they know about what was going on? He wasn't sure. He thought, perhaps, by the time they were his age, there'd be some kind of reckoning. You could only push someone so far before they rose up and demanded some kind of fair shake. For now they were content to scroll on their phones, but would they be content to keep scrolling for another decade? While wages remained the same, while more jobs slipped away overseas to be performed by child slaves and abused workers?

He hoped not, but he wasn't sure.

It was a macro thing, yes, happening all over the world: but there was a sliver of difference in Portland. Maybe more than a sliver, even, although he couldn't quite be sure. There was something peculiar going on in this city. A kind of influence seemed to permeate the air and make little things bigger, and mean things meaner, and ugly things uglier.

Jerry couldn't come close to putting it into words. He couldn't define it scientifically, or point toward it. He couldn't even quite explain to himself what it was that he felt and what it was he was looking for. But there were things that happened in Portland which didn't happen anywhere else.

Take the number of bodies that washed up in the Willamette, for example. Higher than the average across the country by about triple for a river of its size. Take the number of UFO sightings, higher than nearly anywhere else in the world. Or how about the number of missing persons? It wasn't all about the income gap or greed. How about that company—still he wouldn't say the name of it, he valued his life and his job too much for that—which sat on the banks of the river and poured their devilish chemicals into the water and ran their tests on homeless people and...

That'd been his magnum opus. The story to break all stories. He began drafting it nearly 20 years ago, not long after he started at the paper, and he kept at it (always in the dark, always quiet) for years. Running down leads on that one was dangerous. People were getting killed and going missing for asking the questions he was asking. Still, he felt it was an important thing to do. The more mysteries he learned about in Portland, the more evil and dark shit that happened, the more he looked back at that company and their chemicals and their drugs and the tests they were doing. They were like a mountain looming over a little village cast in shadow. Rumors of giants and dragons abounded. But really, it was just the damn mountain, sitting right there in plain sight.

He closed his eyes and sat back.

When he opened them again, they were approaching Vista Bridge. Kids used to call it Suicide Bridge, and for good reason. There were more than a few every year for as long as he could remember. He looked out of the window at it, wondering what peculiar magic pulled at the down and begotten and made them want to look out from that vantage in their last moments.

A red flag swinging from the top of the bridge caught his eye. It was suspended by a rope, centered almost perfectly over the street. Jerry noticed a few cars stopped, staring, and a few folks pointing and talking on the phone. Someone looked disturbed, he thought, and so he looked back again at the flag.

The MAX moved smoothly toward it, and as they neared, he realizes it wasn't a flag at all.

It was the hanging body of a dead man, noosed cleanly around the neck. Not wrapped in a red flag: but wearing a red suit. His feet were bare, and his face was bloodshot, beat red. He was still swinging heavily.

Jerry felt like someone had punched him in the gut. He was

breathless, and suddenly very afraid. Afraid because how many men in red suits were there walking around Portland? How many men who didn't show up for their appointment an hour ago, men who were supposed to have showed up to the appointment in a red suit to talk about a secretive and dangerous organization and...

The MAX shot underneath the swinging red man and he went out of sight. Jerry knew he must have only just died, or else police and fire and ambulance would be swarming the place and, probably, the street would be temporarily shut down. Suicide Bridge blotted out the sun, and for a second, the whole train car was plunged into darkness. No one was speaking: Jerry wasn't even sure if anyone else, absorbed as they were, had noticed.

His heart was beating fast, and he felt a drip of sweat forming on the back of his neck. Was he in danger? Did the man actually kill himself—or was he just another death in the long string of deaths that surrounded his attempt to uncover the truth about the seedy happenings in Portland?

He'd felt like he could be in danger a number of times in his life, but never so much as in this moment. If there was such a thing as a sixth sense, which he thought there probably was, he thought his was telling him, now, that things weren't right.

What did that man in the red suit know? That's what he was wondering now. What information might he have divulged if he'd only been able to hold on long enough, or escape whatever assailants were pursuing him?

Jerry didn't know. And as the train raced out from beneath Vista Bridge, leaving the man in the read suit hanging behind, he wondered if it was best that he didn't.

He had Mary to think of after all, and Denny and Beth. Portland held tight to its secrets. In Portland, the shadows weren't always just a place where light failed to fall. Sometimes they had monsters in them. Sometimes, if you tried to look into the wrong alley or beneath the wrong rock, the things that came squirming out were things that were never meant to be seen.

Jerry leaned back in his seat, closed his eyes, and took a deep breath.

He thought he'd finish the article when he got home. Dot all his I's and cross his T's. He didn't think he could save Portland anymore. It seemed like, maybe, Portland didn't want to be saved. The forces against him were just too big, too many, and too elusive.

Behind his closed eyes, he saw the man in the red suit swinging. He felt lucky to be alive.

THE END

ACKNOWLEDGMENTS

This book is dedicated to those who remember the sounds of the drums reverberating from Waterfront Park to the North Park Blocks.

A special thanks to all artists involved in this project; Ross Malet, Igor Beltrame, Roval Tarroza, Constantine Hlyvlias, Sergey Shirobokov and Anna Vaks. A very special thanks to talented author Tyler Hauth.

Gratitude goes to Mr. Blaine Anarchy, Tyrone Toblerome III, thanks for the milestones and for the vision.

Many thanks for the love and support.

DESIGN & EDITORIAL:
Editor and Creative Director:
ARIKA CHAMBERLAIN

PRODUCTION:
Technical and Production Director:
MR. BLAINE ANARCHY

ISBN:
979-8-9900746-1-3

THIS PAGE IS INTENTIONALLY LEFT BLANK